"How long have you two been seeing each other?"

Logan questioned with infuriating calm.

"Logan." Fighting back tears of frustration, Abby moved away from the door and turned to face him. "I'm asking you to trust me in this. Things are not always what they appear to be." Abby lowered her gaze. This deception hadn't been easy on her. But she was bound by her promise to Tate. She couldn't explain the circumstances of their meeting to Logan and salvage Tate's pride at the same time.

Determinedly Logan started for the door, but Abby's hand delayed him. He paused, his troubled expression revealing the storm raging within him.

"I may be wrong, but I was brought up to believe that love between two people constituted mutual trust," Abby added.

One corner of his mouth quirked upward. "And I assumed, erroneously it seems, that love constituted honesty."

"I . . . I bent the truth a little."

"Why?" he demanded.

"I can't explain now. I may never be able to tell you why. . . ."

Dear Reader,

Although our culture is always changing, the desire to love and be loved is a constant in every woman's heart. Silhouette Romances reflect that desire, sweeping you away with books that will make you laugh and cry, poignant stories that will move you time and time again.

This year we're featuring Romances with a playful twist. Remember those fun-loving heroines who always manage to get themselves into tricky predicaments? You'll enjoy reading about their escapades in Silhouette Romances by Brittany Young, Debbie Macomber, Annette Broadrick and Rita Rainville.

We're also publishing Romances by many of your all-time favorites such as Ginna Gray, Diana Palmer and Joan Hohl. Your overwhelming reaction to these authors has served as a touchstone for us, and we're pleased to bring you more books with Silhouette's distinctive medley of charm, wit and—above all—*romance*. I hope you enjoy this book, and the many stories to come.

Sincerely,

Rosalind Noonan
Senior Editor
SILHOUETTE BOOKS

DEBBIE MACOMBER
Laughter in the Rain

Silhouette *Romance*

Published by Silhouette Books New York

America's Publisher of Contemporary Romance

To Tami Sahli, with love and appreciation

SILHOUETTE BOOKS
300 E. 42nd St., New York, N.Y.   10017

Copyright © 1986 by Debbie Macomber

ISBN: 0-373-08437-4

First Silhouette Books printing June 1986

America's Publisher of Contemporary Romance

Printed in the U.S.A.

Books by Debbie Macomber

Silhouette Special Edition

Starlight #128
Borrowed Dreams #241
Reflections of Yesterday #284

Silhouette Romance

That Wintery Feeling #316
Promise Me Forever #341
Adam's Image #349
The Trouble with Caasi #379
A Friend or Two #392
Christmas Masquerade #405
Shadow Chasing #415
Yesterday's Hero #426
Laughter in the Rain #437

DEBBIE MACOMBER

has quickly become one of Silhouette's most prolific authors. As a wife and mother of four, she not only manages to keep her family happy, but she also keeps her publisher and readers happy with each book she writes.

MINNESOTA
IOWA

CANADA

LAKE SUPERIOR

NORTH DAKOTA

MINNESOTA

Minneapolis

WISCONSIN

SOUTH DAKOTA

IOWA

NEBRASKA

Des Moines

ILLINOIS

MISSOURI

Chapter One

I'm late, so late."

The words repeated themselves in Abby Carpenter's mind with every frantic push of the bike pedal. She was late. A worried glance at her watch when she paused at the traffic light confirmed that Mai-Ling would already be in Diamond Lake Park, wondering where Abby was. Abby should have known better than to try on that lovely silk blouse, but she had seen it in the store's display window and couldn't resist. Now she was paying for the impulse. And God knows she was impulsive.

The light turned green and Abby peddled furiously, rounding the corner to the park entrance at breakneck speed.

Panting, she pulled to an abrupt stop in front of the bike stand and secured the lock of her ten-speed around a concrete post. Hurriedly, she ran across the lush green lawn where she normally met Mai-Ling. A rush of relief washed through her when she spotted the Oriental woman.

Mai-Ling had recently immigrated to Minneapolis from Hong Kong. As a volunteer for the World Literary Movement, Abby was helping the petite Oriental learn to read English. Light honey-colored skin, warm brown eyes and a small mouth that formed into a sweet smile greeted Abby from across the park. The beautiful Chinese woman waved eagerly. Abby had been meeting weekly with Mai-Ling for only two months and already felt a deep respect for the young woman's determination to master the English language.

"I'm sorry I'm late," Abby apologized breathlessly as she tucked a strand of chestnut-colored hair around her ear.

Mai-Ling shrugged one shoulder. "No problem," she said with a crooked smile.

The words and gesture demonstrated how quickly her friend was adapting to the American way of life.

To hide her giggles, Mai-Ling placed a cupped palm over her mouth.

"What's so funny?" Abby questioned as she slid the backpack off her left shoulder and set it on the picnic table.

"You wear funny two shocks," Mai-Ling mumbled, lowering her eyes to avoid looking into Abby's.

"Funny two shocks?" Abby repeated, not understanding until Mai-Ling directed her gaze to Abby's legs. A self-derisive smile touched her lips as she viewed one red knee-high and one blue knee-high sock.

"Oh dear," Abby sighed disgustedly and sat on the table bench. "I was in such a rush I didn't even notice." No wonder the salesclerk had given her a funny look.

"I laugh with you," Mai-Ling continued in painstaking English.

Abby understood what her friend was saying. Mai-Ling wanted to be sure that Abby realized she wasn't laughing *at* her. "I know, my friend," she said as she zipped open the backpack and took out several thin books.

Mai-Ling sat opposite Abby. "The man's here again," she murmured.

"Man?" Abby twisted around. "What man?"

Abby couldn't believe she'd been so unobservant. She experienced a slight twinge of apprehension as her expressive blue eyes rested on the tall stranger. There was something vaguely familiar about him that bothered her. He was the same man she'd seen yesterday afternoon in the grocery store. Oh, good heaven's, had he been following her? Certainly she'd be aware of it if someone was. She adored Dashiell Hammett and loved a good mystery. That should prove something.

The stranger turned and leaned against a tree not more than twenty feet away, granting her a full view of his face. His tawny hair gleamed under the soft glow of the sun that filtered through the leaves of the huge elm. Beneath thick brows were deeply-set brown eyes. Even from this distance Abby could see that they were intense. His rugged face seemed carved with abrupt angles and planes. But he was attractive in an earthy way that would appeal to a lot of women. Abby was no exception.

"He was here last week," Mai-Ling insisted. "I'm sure it's the same man."

"Funny, I don't remember seeing him," she murmured, unable to disguise her discomfort.

"I wouldn't worry. He's a nice man. The animals like him."

"Then I won't worry either," Abby said with a light shrug as she handed Mai-Ling the first workbook.

In addition to being observant, Mai-Ling was a beautiful, sensitive and highly intelligent woman. Sometimes she became angry and frustrated at her inability to communicate, but Abby was astonished at the young woman's phenomenal progress. Mai-Ling had mastered the English alphabet in only a few hours and was reading Level Two books.

A couple of times while Mai-Ling was reading a primer story about a woman applying for her first job, Abby's attention drifted to the tall stranger. Amazed, she watched as he coaxed a squirrel down the trunk of the tree. He pulled something from his pocket and within seconds the small creature was eating out of his hand. As if aware of Abby's scrutiny, he stood up and sauntered lazily to the lake. The instant he appeared, the ducks squawked as though recognizing an old friend. The tall man took bread crumbs from a sack he carried and fed the birds. Lowering himself to their level, he threw back his head and laughed as if he understood their loud chatter.

An involuntary smile lifted the soft line of Abby's mouth. Mai-Ling was right: this man had a way with wildlife—and women, too, if her pounding heart was anything to judge by.

A few times Mai-Ling faltered over a word, and Abby paused to help her.

The hour sped past quickly, and before either was aware, it was time for the young woman to meet her bus. Abby walked with Mai-Ling to the busy street and waited until she had boarded. The Chinese woman cheerfully waved to Abby from the back of the bus.

Peddling her ten-speed toward her apartment, Abby's thoughts again drifted to the tall, good-looking stranger. He enthralled her. Obviously he was attracted to her if he continued to come to the park each week. But he certainly didn't look like the shy type and Abby wondered at his game. Maybe it wasn't she who attracted him; perhaps it was Mai-Ling. No, she dismissed the thought as quickly as it came. Even Mai-Ling had noticed the way the handsome stranger had studied Abby. He was interested in her. Great, she mused contentedly; Logan Fletcher could do with some competition.

Humming the theme song from *Hawaii Five-O*, Abby pulled into the parking lot of her apartment building, threw her leg over the side of her bike and climbed off. Automatically she reached for her backpack to get the apartment key. Her hand sliced through the air; her backpack wasn't there. Surprised, Abby turned in short circles, certain it was somewhere. It had to be. Only it wasn't. Obviously she'd left it at the park. Oh great! She exhaled in frustration and turned, prepared to pedal the mile to the park and retrieve her backpack.

"Looking for this?" A deep male voice startled Abby and her heart almost dropped to her knees, then bounced to her throat. The ten-speed slipped out from under her and she staggered a few steps before regaining her balance.

"Don't you know better than to sneak up on someone like that? I could have..." The words died on her lips as she whirled around, hands placed defiantly on her hips, and faced the good-looking stranger. With her mouth hanging half open she stared into the deepest pair of brown eyes she'd ever seen: the man from the park.

Her tongue-tied antics seemed to amuse him, but then it could have been her mismatched socks. "You forgot this." He handed her the backpack. Speechless, Abby took it and hugged it against her stomach. She felt grateful and awkward. She started to thank him when abruptly another thought came to mind.

"How'd...how'd you know where I live?" The words came out tight and slightly scratchy. Jack Lord never sounded like this.

The abrupt planes and angles of his face sharpened. "I've frightened you, haven't I?"

"How'd you know?" she repeated the question less aggressively. He hadn't scared her. If anything, she felt a startling attraction to the sheer force of his gruff masculinity. Logan would be shocked. Logan nothing— Abby was stupefied.

His hands tightened into fists. "I followed you."

"Oh." A thousand confused emotions butted against the corners of her mind. He was so good-looking that Abby couldn't force out another word.

"I didn't mean to scare you," he said with tight impatience. Abby sensed that if he was angry, it was with himself.

"You didn't," she hurried to assure him. "I have an active imagination."

Impatiently, he rammed his hands deep into pants pockets. "I'll leave before I do any more damage."

"Please don't apologize. I should be thanking you. There's a Coke machine around the corner. Would you like to—"

"I've done enough for one day." Abruptly he turned away.

"At least tell me your name?" Abby didn't know where the question came from; it tumbled from her lips without her even having formed the thought.

"Tate." He tossed the information over his shoulder as he stalked away. Just the way he strode conjured up the image of an untamed beast. His long strides hinted at unrestrained power and the indomitable strength of a jungle cat.

"Goodbye, Tate," she called, before he opened his car door. When he glanced her way, she lifted her hand and wiggled her fingers. "And thanks."

A smile curved over his handsome features. "I like your socks," he returned.

Pointedly she looked down at the mismatched pair. "I'm starting a new trend," she said with a short laugh.

Standing outside her apartment door, Abby waited until Tate started the car engine and drove away.

Later that night, Logan picked her up and they had hamburgers and afterward went to the most recent Ron Howard movie. Logan's obligatory good-night kiss was . . . pleasant. That was the only way Abby knew how to describe it. Abby had the impression Logan kissed her because he always kissed her good-night. To her dismay, she admitted that there had never been any driving urgency behind his kisses. They'd been dating almost a year and the mysterious Tate was capable of stirring more emotion in her with a three-minute conversation than Logan had the entire evening. Abby wasn't exactly sure why they continued to date each other. They worked in the same building, shared the same friends, but their relationship was in a rut. The time had come to add a little spice to her life and Abby knew exactly where the spice would be coming from—Tate.

After Logan left, Abby settled into the thick overstuffed chair that had once belonged to her grandfather, and picked up a Steven King thriller.

Dano, her silvery-eyed cat, crawled into her lap as Abby opened the book. Absently she stroked the length of the animal. Her hand froze in midstroke as she discovered the hero's name: Logan. Slightly unnerved, she set the book aside and jumped up from the chair to turn on the television. She shouldn't feel guilty because she felt attracted to another man. The television screen came into focus just in time for Logan Furniture to announce its once-a-year sofa sale. Abby stared at the flashing name and testily switched off the dial. This was crazy! Logan wouldn't care if she were interested in another man. He might even be grateful. Their relationship was based on mutual friendship and had progressed to simple routine. If Abby were attracted to another man, Logan would be the first to step aside. He was like that—warm, unselfish and an all-around good sport.

Her troubled thoughts Saturday were only the beginning. Tate dominated every waking minute, which only went to prove that her social life was sadly lacking. Logan was great, but Abby longed for some excitement. He was so staid—yes, that was the word—*staid*. Solid as a rock, but about as imaginative as a vanilla ice cream.

Logan stopped at her apartment Sunday afternoon, which was no surprise. He always came over on Sunday afternoon. That was his problem; Logan didn't have much of an imagination. They usually did something together. Nothing all that exciting. More often than not Abby went over to his house and cooked their dinner. Sometimes they played backgammon, but he usually won. During the summer they'd often ride their ten-speeds around the park. Some of their most stimulating dates had been spent in Diamond Lake Park. Logan would lie across the grass and rest his head in her lap while he chewed on a long stem of grass.

They'd been seeing each other so often that the last time they'd had dinner at her parents, Abby's father had suggested it was time they thought about getting married. Abby had been mortified. Logan was wonderful— Abby couldn't deny that—but he tended to be somewhat dull. Her mother had tactfully reminded Abby later that Logan may not win any Mr. Universe awards, but he was her best prospect. Abby couldn't see any reason to rush into marriage. She had plenty of time to pick and choose.

"I thought we'd bike-ride around the park," Logan suggested.

The day was gloriously sunny and although Abby faulted Logan's lack of imagination, the idea was appealing. She enjoyed the feel of the breeze running through her hair and the sense of exhilaration that came with the exercise.

"Hi," Abby and Logan were greeted by Patty Martin just inside the park's boundaries. "How's it going?"

"Fine," Logan answered for them as they braked to a stop. "How about you?"

Patty had recently started to work in the same office complex as Logan and Abby. Although Abby didn't know the girl well, she'd learned that Patty was living with her married sister. The two girls had talked briefly at lunch one day and Abby wanted to strengthen the friendship.

"I'm fine too," Patty answered shyly and looked away.

"Great." In some ways the girl reminded Abby of Mai-Ling. The young Oriental girl hadn't said more than a few words to Abby the first couple of weeks they'd worked together. Only as they came to know each other did Mai-Ling blossom. Abby had never been shy. The world was her friend and she felt certain Patty would

blossom the same way once she was comfortable with
Abby.

"I can't talk now. I saw you and just wanted to say
hello. Have fun, you two," Patty murmured and hurried
away.

Confused, Abby watched her leave. The girl looked
like a frightened mouse as she scurried across the plush
lawn. The description was more than apt. Patty's drab
brown hair was pulled away from her face and styled un-
attractively. She didn't wear makeup and was so shy that
it was difficult to strike up a conversation.

After biking around the lake a couple of times, they
stopped and got something cool to drink. Resting, Logan slipped an affectionate arm across Abby's shoulders. "Have I told you that you're lovely today?"

The compliment surprised Abby; there were times she
was convinced Logan didn't notice anything about her.
"Thank you. I might add that you're looking rather
debonair yourself," she said with twinkling eyes, then
added, "but I won't. No need for us both to get a big
head."

Logan smiled absently as they walked their bikes out
of the park. His look was more distant than she could
remember. In some ways he hadn't been himself lately,
but she couldn't put her finger on anything specific.

"Do you mind if we call our afternoon short?" he
asked unexpectedly.

He didn't offer an explanation, which surprised Abby.
They'd spent most Sunday afternoons together for the
past year. More surprising was the fact that Abby realized she really didn't care. "No, that shouldn't be any
problem. I've got a ton of laundry to do anyway."

They talked for a couple of minutes longer before
climbing on their bikes and riding back to Abby's apart-

ment. Abby spent the remainder of her afternoon doing her fingernails, feeling lazy and ignoring her laundry. She talked to her mother on the phone and promised to stop by sometime that week. At twenty-two, Abby had been on her own a year and a half. Her job as receptionist had developed with time and specialized training into a position as an X-ray technician for an orthopedic surgeon. The advancement had included a healthy pay increase— enough for her to take the plunge into her own apartment, which she loved. For a time, Abby had considered finding a roommate, but had rejected the idea. For the first time in her life she was utterly on her own, and she relished the independence.

Several times over the next few days, Abby discovered her thoughts drifting to Tate. Their encounter had been brief, but impressionable. He was the most exciting thing that had happened to her in months.

"What's the matter with you?" Abby admonished herself while studying her reflection in the mirror. "A handsome man gives you a little attention and you don't know how to act."

Dano mewed loudly and weaved himself between her bare legs, his long tail tickling her calves. It was the middle of June and already the hot summer weather had arrived.

"I wasn't talking to you." She leaned over and petted the cat. "And don't tell me you're hungry. I know better."

"Meow."

"You've already had your dinner."

"Meow. Meow."

"Don't you talk to me in that tone of voice again. You hear?"

"Meow."

Abby tossed him the catnip mouse he loved to hurl in the air and chase after madly. Logan had gotten Dano the toy mouse. With his nose in the air, and obviously out of joint, the fussy cat ignored the toy and sauntered into Abby's room and went out the open window. In some obscure way, Abby felt that she was doing the same thing to Logan and experienced a pang of guilt.

"And don't come back until you're in a better frame of mind," Abby shouted irritably after him.

To create a crosscurrent of air in the stuffy apartment, Abby opened the front door and locked the screen. Settling in the large overstuffed chair, she looped one leg over the arm and munched on an apple as she read. She was so engrossed in the suspense thriller that when she glanced at her watch, her eyes rounded with surprise. Her calligraphy class was in half an hour and Logan would arrive in less than fifteen minutes. Logan was as punctual as a Swiss clock, and although he seldom said anything, she could tell by the tight set of his mouth how much he disliked it when she was behind schedule.

The "I'm late, I'm late" theme ran through her mind as she vaulted out of the chair, changed pants and rammed her right foot into her tennis shoe without untying the lace. Whipping a brush through the long length of her brown hair she searched frantically for the other shoe.

"It's got to be here," she told the empty room frantically. "Dano," she cried out in frustration. "Did you take my shoe?"

On her knees she crawled across the carpet, desperately tossing aside whatever happened to cross her path— a week-old newspaper, a scarf, the mismatched pair of socks from last Saturday and a variety of other unimportant items.

"Missing something?" Tate's husky voice came from the other side of the screen.

Abby felt the hot color seep up from her neck and flower in her cheeks. He would come now when she was least expecting him, when she wasn't prepared and looking her worst. "Hello again." Her voice sounded unnaturally high. Standing, she bit into the corner of her bottom lip and tried to smile. "My shoe's gone."

"Walked away, is that it?"

His teasing coaxed a smile. "You might say that. It was here a few minutes ago. I was reading and..." She dropped to her knees and lifted the skirting that went around the chair. There, in all its glory, was the shoe.

"Find it?"

"Yes." She sat on the edge of the cushion and jerked her foot into the shoe.

"It might help if you untie the laces," he said from the other side of the screen, watching her with those marvelous eyes.

"I know, but I'm in a hurry." With her heel crushing the back of the shoe, Abby hobbled to the door and unhooked the lock.

"Abby?"

"Yes," she opened the screen and offered him her hand.

He took it in his and smiled. "Is it Miss or Mrs.?"

A tingling sensation skirted up her arm at the touch of his hand as it folded over hers. At the same time a lump filled her throat.

"Miss," she managed finally. Dear heaven, she was acting like a tongue-tied teenager trying to hide the fact she was wearing braces. But Abby wasn't a teen and her teeth had been straight for years. Tate's hand was callused and rough from work. She successfully restrained the desire to turn it over and examine the palm. His handsome face was tanned from exposure to the elements and instinctively Abby realized that the darkened color of his skin didn't come from any sunlamp. Tate was handsome, compellingly so.

"It looks as if I came at an inconvenient time."

"Oh, no," she hurried to assure him. "I wasn't doing anything special," she lied. For the first time she noticed that he'd released his grip while she continued to hold her hand in midair. Self-consciously she let go of his hand and lowered hers to her side. "Sit down," she said, motioning toward her favorite chair. The hot color in her face threatened to suffocate her with its intensity.

Tate sat and lazily crossed his legs, apparently unaware of the effect he had on her.

This overwhelming reaction shocked Abby. She had dated several men. Nor was she naive or stupid. "Would you like something to drink?" she asked as she hastily retreated to the kitchen, not waiting for his answer. Pausing, she frantically prayed that for once, just once, Logan would be late. No sooner had the thought formed when there was a loud knock on the screen door.

"Abby?"

Logan. Abby cringed inwardly.

Tate had stood and opened the door by the time she turned around. The two men eyed one another skeptically. A slight frown drew Logan's brows together in a single, tight line.

"Logan, this is Tate. Tate, Logan Fletcher." Abby flushed uncomfortably and darted an apologetic look at them both.

"I thought we had a class tonight," Logan said somewhat defensively.

"This is my fault," Tate supplied, his gaze resting on Abby's face and for one heart-stopping moment on her softly parted lips. "I dropped by unexpectedly."

Logan's mouth thinned with displeasure and Abby pulled her eyes from Tate's. Logan had never been the jealous type, but then there had never been the opportunity for him to reveal that side of his nature. It surprised her now. Abby had been having too much fun with life to be serious about any one man. Logan had understood and accepted that, or so she thought.

"I'll come back another time," Tate suggested. "Logan's got prior claim to your company tonight."

"We're taking classes together," Abby rushed to explain. "I'm taking calligraphy and Logan's studying chess. We drive there together, that's all."

Tate's attention shifted back to her. His smile was understanding. "I won't keep you."

"Nice to have met you," Logan stated as if he meant exactly the opposite.

Tate turned back and nodded with hard amusement. "Perhaps we'll meet again."

Logan nodded like a warlord challenged to a duel. "Perhaps."

The minute Tate left Abby whirled around to face Logan. "That was a rotten way to behave," she whispered fiercely. "For heaven's sake—you were acting like you owned me . . . like I was your property."

"Think about it, Abby," Logan returned just as forcefully, also in a heated whisper. His dark eyes narrowed as he stalked to the other side of the room. "We've been dating steadily for almost a year. I assumed that in that time you would have developed some loyalty. Obviously I was mistaken."

"Loyalty? Is that all our relationship means to you?" she demanded hotly.

Logan didn't answer her. He walked to the screen door and held it open, indicating that if she was coming the time was now. Silently Abby followed him to the parking lot.

The entire way to the community center they sat like statues, neither speaking, their attention centered directly in front of them. The hard set of Logan's mouth indicated the tight reign he had on his temper. Abby forced her expression to remain haughtily cold and proud.

They parted in the hallway, Logan taking the first left while Abby continued down the hall. A couple of the gals she had become friends with greeted her with cheery smiles. Abby had difficulty responding, taking twice as long as normal to set up her supplies.

The class didn't go well, since Abby's attention kept drifting to the scene with Tate and Logan. Logan was obviously jealous. He'd revealed more emotion in those few minutes with Tate than in the past twelve months. Logan tended to be serious and somber, while she was flighty and fun-loving. They were simply a mismatched couple. Like her socks: one red, one blue. Logan had become too comfortable these past months. The time had come for a change, and after tonight he was sure to recognize that.

They normally met in the coffee shop beside the parking lot after class. Logan was already in a booth when she arrived.

Wordlessly, Abby slipped into the seat opposite him. Folding her hands on the Formica top, she pretended to study her nails, wondering if Logan was ever going to speak. This was ridiculous; they were both behaving like children.

"Why are you so angry?" Abby spoke first, disliking the tense silence that stretched between them. "I hardly know Tate. We only met a few days ago."

"How many times have you gone out with him?"

"None," Abby replied tightly.

"But not because you turned him down," Logan stated and shook his head grimly. "I saw the way you looked at him, Abby. It was all you could do to keep from drooling."

"That's not true," she denied vehemently and realized he was probably right. She had never done a good job of hiding her feelings. "I admit I find him attractive but—"

"But what?" Logan taunted softly. "But you had this old boyfriend you had to get rid of first."

"I've never held the fact that you're thirty against you, Logan, and you know it." Blue fire blazed from her eyes.

The hint of a smile touched his full mouth. "I wasn't referring to my age. I was pointing to the fact that we've been seeing each other two, sometimes three times a week and suddenly you're not so sure of how you feel about me."

Abby opened, then closed her mouth. Logan had hit the nail right on the proverbial head.

"That's it, isn't it?"

"Logan." She said his name on a sigh, regretting everything. "I like you. You must realize that. Over the past year I've grown very... fond of you."

"Fond?" He spat the word at her as if he found the taste of it bitter. "One is fond of cats or dogs—not men. And most particularly not me."

"All right, all right," Abby agreed. "That was a bad choice of words."

"You're not exactly sure what you feel." Logan said, issuing the comment softly, almost under his breath.

Abby's fingers knotted until she could feel the pain in her hands. Logan was right, she didn't know. She was attracted to Tate, but she didn't know anything beyond his first name. The problem was that what she saw she liked. If her feelings for Logan were what they should be after a year's time, she wouldn't want Tate to ask her out so badly. At least she didn't think she would.

"You don't know, do you," Logan stated again.

Sadly, her head hanging so that her oval face was framed in a wreath of dark hair, Abby shook her head. "I don't want to hurt you," she murmured softly.

"You're not." Logan's hand reached across the width of the table and squeezed her fingers reassuringly. "Beyond anything else, we're friends and I don't want to do anything to upset that friendship because it's important to me."

"That's important to me, too," she said and offered him a feeble smile. Their eyes met as the waitress came and turned over the beige cups and filled them with steaming liquid.

"Do you want a menu tonight?"

Abby couldn't have eaten anything and slowly shook her head.

"Not tonight. Thanks anyway," Logan answered for them.

"I don't deserve you," Abby said after the waitress had moved to the next booth.

For the first time all night Logan's lips curved into a genuine smile. "That's something I don't want you to forget."

Abby studied him while they sipped their coffee. Holding the cup with both hands, she blew into the side of the steaming mug and took another sip. Logan's eyes were as brown as Tate's. Funny she hadn't remembered how brown they were. Tonight the color was intense, keener than she could ever remember. They made quite a couple: she was such a scatterbrain and he was so unemotional. Logan's jaw was well-defined. Proud. Tate's jaw, although different, revealed that same quality—determination. With Logan, Abby recognized there wasn't anything he couldn't do if he wanted. Instinctively she realized the same was true for Tate.

It was unfair that one man she'd seen only a couple of times could affect her this way. If she fell madly in love with someone, it should be Logan.

"You're looking thoughtful." His words broke into her troubled thoughts.

"Sorry." Abby lowered her gaze.

"You didn't even add sugar to your coffee."

Abby made a funny face. "No wonder it tastes so awful."

Chuckling, he handed her the sugar.

Pouring the white granules onto the spoon, Abby stirred the sweetener into her coffee. Logan had a nice mouth. She couldn't remember thinking that in a long time. She had when they'd first met, but that was nearly two years ago. She glanced up to watch him smooth the thick brown hair along the side of his head. He was so— Abby searched for the right word—together. Nothing ever seemed to rattle Logan. There wasn't an obstacle he couldn't overcome with cool reason. She hated that. For once, just once, Abby wanted him to do something crazy and nonsensical and fun.

"Logan." She spoke softly, coaxingly. "Let's drive to Des Moines tonight."

He looked at her as if she were crazy. "Des Moines, Iowa?"

"Yes. Wouldn't it be fun just to take off and drive and drive for hours and turn around and come home?"

"That's not fun, that's torture."

Abby pressed her lips together and nodded. She shouldn't have asked. She'd known his answer even before he spoke.

The ride home was as silent as the drive to class. The tension wasn't nearly as straining, but it was still evident.

"I have the feeling you're angry," Logan said as he parked in front of her apartment building. "I'm sorry that spending the entire night on the road doesn't appeal to me. I've got this silly need for sleep. From what I understand, it affects several older citizens."

"I'm not angry," Abby said firmly. She felt disappointed, but not angry.

Logan's hand caressed her cheek, curving around her neck and directing her mouth to his. Abby closed her eyes expecting the usual feather-light kiss. Instead, Logan pulled her gently into the shelter of his arms and kissed her soundly. The pressure of his mouth parted her lips as his tongue sought hers. Surprised, but delighted, Abby groaned softly, liking what he was doing. Her hands slipped over his shoulders and joined at the base of his neck.

Logan had never kissed her with such intensity, such unrestrained need. His mouth moved over hers, teasing her with short, biting kisses while his hands roamed over her back and under her light cotton top, seeking her breasts. Abby sucked in a startled breath at the pure sensation that shot through her. When he released her, Abby sighed longingly and rested her head against the muscular cushion of his chest. Involuntarily a picture of Tate entered her mind. This was what she had imagined kissing him would be like. Not Logan.

"You were pretending I was Tate, weren't you?" he whispered against her hair.

Chapter Two

Oh, Logan, of course I wasn't,'' Abby answered somewhat guiltily. She had thought of Tate, but she hadn't pretended Logan's kiss was Tate's.

He brushed his face along the side of her hair, tangling the silky tendrils.

Abby was certain he wanted to say something more, but he didn't, remaining silent as he climbed out of the car and walked around to her side. She smiled weakly as he offered her his hand. Logan could be such a gentleman. She was perfectly capable of getting out of a car herself, but he wouldn't allow it. Not when he was there to help her. Abby supposed she should be grateful, but she wasn't.

Lightly, he kissed her again outside her front door. Letting herself inside, Abby was aware that Logan waited on the other side of the wooden door until he heard her turn the lock.

After changing into her long nylon nightgown, Abby went into the kitchen and poured a tall glass of milk. She sat at the small round table and brought her feet up to the edge of the chair and pulled her gown over her knees. Did she love Logan? The realization came almost immediately. Although he'd taken offense, "fond" had aptly described her feelings. She liked Logan, but Tate had aroused far more emotion in her during their short acquaintance. Downing the milk, Abby turned off the light and miserably decided to go to bed.

Saturday afternoon, Abby arrived at the park a half-hour early, hoping Tate would be there and they'd have a chance to talk. She hadn't heard from him and wondered if he'd decided Logan had a prior claim to her affection. However, Tate didn't look like the type who would easily be discouraged. She found him almost immediately in the same spot as last week and waved happily.

"I was hoping you'd be here," she said eagerly and sat on the grass beside him, leaning her back against the massive tree trunk.

"My thoughts exactly," Tate replied, with a warm smile that staggered Abby's heart rate.

"I'm sorry about Logan," she murmured, weaving her fingers through the grass.

"There's no need to apologize."

"But he was such a boor," Abby returned, feeling guilty for being so unkind.

Tate cast her a look of surprise. "He didn't behave any differently than I would have, had the circumstances been reversed."

"Logan doesn't own me," she returned defiantly.

A smile bracketed the edges of his sensuous mouth. "That's one piece of news I'm glad to hear."

Their eyes met and he smiled. Abby could feel her bones melt. It was all she could do to smile back.

"Do you like roller-skating?"

"I love it." She hadn't skated since she was a teen at the local roller rink, but if Tate suggested they stand on their heads in the middle of the road, Abby would have happily agreed.

"Would you like to meet me here tomorrow afternoon?"

"Sure," she said without hesitating. "Here?" she repeated, sitting up.

"You have skated?" He gave her a worried glance.

"Oh, sure." Abby had forgotten how popular it had become to make the rounds through the park. She'd viewed several skaters, wearing earphones and listening to a local rock station as they flew along the paths with a skill that was astonishing. "Tomorrow?" Her voice went squeaky.

"Is that a problem?"

"No, I'll be here. What time?"

"Three," Tate suggested. "Afterward we'll go out for something to eat."

"This sounds better all the time," Abby teased.

"Don't tell me you're one of those women who can eat a man to the poorhouse."

"All right, I won't tell you." An impish smile formed deep dimples in her flushed cheeks. "But be warned, I do have a healthy appetite. Logan says—" she nearly choked on the name, immediately wishing she could draw it back.

"You were saying something about Logan," Tate prompted.

"Not really." She gave a light shrug and flushed involuntarily.

Mai-Ling stepped off the bus and Abby stood up. Brushing the grass from her legs, she smiled warmly at her friend.

"Why do you meet the girl?" Tate asked. The teasing light vanished from his eyes and was replaced by something more than normal curiosity. They grew dark and intense, more serious than she'd ever seen them.

"I do volunteer work with the World Literary Movement. Mai-Ling can read perfectly in Chinese, but she's an American now so I'm helping her learn to read and write English."

"Have you been a volunteer long?"

"A couple of years now. Why? Would you like to help? We're always looking for able-bodied volunteers."

"Me?" He looked stunned and more than a little shocked. "Not now. I've got more than I can handle helping at the zoo."

"The zoo?" Abby shot back excitedly. "Are you a volunteer?"

"The zoo refers to it as a docent."

"Is there a difference?"

"A small one," Tate said as he stood, and glanced at his watch. "I'll explain more about it tomorrow. Right now I've got to get back to work before the boss discovers why I've taken extended lunch breaks the past four Saturdays."

"I'll look forward to tomorrow," Abby murmured, thinking she'd never known anyone as compelling as Tate.

"You met the man?" Mai-Ling asked as she sauntered to Abby's side and followed Abby's gaze to the retreating male figure.

"Yes, I met him," Abby answered wistfully, her eyes full of stars. "Oh, Mai-Ling, I think I'm in love!"

"Love?" Mai-Ling returned, disgusted. "American word for love is bad."

"Bad?" Abby repeated, not completely comprehending what her friend was saying.

"Yes. In English the word for 'love' says all."

Abby turned her attention from Tate to the woman and asked, "How do you mean?"

"In America love for a husband is the same as love for chocolate. I hear a lady on bus say she love chocolate, then say she in love with new man," Mai-Ling breathed in astonishment and disbelief. "In Chinese it is much different. Much better."

"No doubt you're right," Abby said with a bemused grin. It hadn't taken Abby long as a volunteer to discover the shortcomings of the English language.

"You will see the man again?"

"Tomorrow," Abby said dreamily. Suddenly her eyes widened. Tomorrow was Sunday, and Logan would be expecting her to do something with him. Oh dear, this was turning out to be a disaster. Not only hadn't she skated in years, but she was bound to have another uncomfortable confrontation with Logan. The eager anticipation for the morrow was quickly substituted by a sinking feeling in the pit of her stomach.

Abby spent a miserable night. She'd attempted to phone Logan and make up an excuse about not being able to get together this Sunday, but he hadn't been home. Consequently her sleep was fitful and intermittent. It wasn't that Logan called and arranged a time each week; they had a simple understanding that Sundays were their day. Abby couldn't remember a week when they hadn't done something. Her sudden decision would be as readable as the morning headlines. Logan would know she was meeting Tate.

Abby's first inclination was not to be there when he arrived, but that was the coward's way out. In addition, Abby knew Logan well enough to realize that her attempts to dodge him wouldn't work. Either he'd go to the park and look for her there or drive to her parents' and worry them sick.

By the time he did arrive, Abby's stomach felt like a lead balloon had settled inside.

"Beautiful afternoon, isn't it?" Logan came over to her and slipped an arm around her waist, drawing her close to his side. So many times in the past year, Abby had longed for him to hold her like this, to stake his claim to her heart. Now when he did, she wanted to scream with frustration. "What would you like to do?" he asked, nuzzling her neck and holding her close.

"Logan," Abby hesitated, and cleared her throat, fighting the desire to cry out with guilt and frustration. "I've got other plans this afternoon." Her voice didn't even sound like her own as she squeezed her eyes closed, afraid to meet his hard gaze.

A grimness stole into his eyes as his hand tightened. "You're meeting Tate, aren't you?"

Abby caught her breath at the ferocity of his tone, low and filled with anger. "Of course not." She couldn't look at him. For the first time in their relationship, Abby was blatantly lying to Logan. No wonder she was experiencing this terrible guilty feeling. For one crazy minute, Abby felt like bursting into tears and running out of the apartment.

"Tell me what you're doing then," he demanded with barely disguised irritation.

His eyes narrowed as Abby struggled with regret. She swallowed at the painful knot blocking her throat. "You cut our time together short last week and I didn't demand to know where you were going. I don't feel it's too much to expect the same courtesy."

Logan's grip on her waist slackened, but he didn't release her. "What about later? Couldn't we meet for dinner? There's something I wanted to discuss."

"I can't," she said quickly. Too quickly. Telltale color warmed her face.

Logan studied her for a long moment and then dropped his arm, freeing her from his touch. She should have been glad. Instead she felt chilled and suddenly bereft.

"Let me know when you're free." His words were as cold as a blast of wind off an Arctic sea. He started to move toward the door.

"Logan," Abby called out to him desperately. "Don't be angry. Please."

He paused and turned around. His hard gaze flickered over her briefly. Wordlessly, he turned and left.

Abby wanted to crawl into a hole, curl up and die. Logan deserved so much better than this. Any number of women would call her a fool—and rightly so.

Dressed in white linen shorts and a red cotton shirt, Abby studied her reflection in the full-length mirror on the back of the bedroom door. Her hair hung in long pigtails that danced off her upper arms. If she was going to behave like a child then she might as well dress like one. Cosmetics did little to disguise the doubt and unhappiness in her eyes. Releasing a jagged breath, Abby tied the sleeves of a sweater around her neck and headed out the door.

Tate was standing at the elm tree waiting for her when she arrived. He was dressed casually in jeans and a V-neck sweater that hinted at a mass of curly chest hair.

Even across the distance of the park, Abby recognized the quiet authority of the man. His virile look attracted the attention of other women in the vicinity, but Tate didn't seem to notice.

He smiled and started walking toward her, his look approving as he surveyed her long legs and rounded but narrow hips.

"You look like you've lost your best friend," Tate said as he slipped a casual arm around her shoulder. "Problem?"

"Not really." Her voice thinned to a quiver, and she managed to give him a broad smile. "I'm hoping we can rent skates. I don't have a pair."

"We can."

It didn't take long for Tate's infectious good mood to brighten Abby's spirits. Soon she was laughing at her bungling attempts to roller-skate. A concrete pathway was astonishingly different from the smooth, polished surface of the roller rink. Either that, or it had been longer than she realized since her last time on skates.

Tate tucked a hand along the side of her hip as his movements guided hers.

"You're doing great." His eyes were smiling as he relaxed his grip.

Laughing, Abby looked away from the pathway to answer him when her skate hit a rut and she tumbled forward, wildly thrashing her arms at her side in an effort to remain upright. She would have fallen if Tate hadn't been holding her. His hand tightened, bringing her intimately closer. Her skate faltered a bit from the effect of his nearness.

"I'm a natural."

"A natural klutz," he finished for her.

They skated for two hours. When Tate suggested they stop, Abby glanced at her wristwatch and was amazed at the time.

"Hungry?" Tate asked next.

"Famished." Abby was surprised how accurate the description was. "I hope you brought your bankbook."

"I prefer to deal with cash."

The hamburger place Tate took her to was one of those fancy places that charged an enormous sum for atmosphere, but where the reputation for the food was well-earned. Abby couldn't imagine Logan bringing her someplace like this. Knowing that made the outing all the more enticing.

When the waitress came Abby ordered the avocado burger with a large stuffed baked potato and strawberry shortcake for dessert.

Tate looked taken aback. "I'll have the same," he told the waitress, who wrote down their order and stepped away from the table. "Is your appetite always this healthy?"

"Always!" She bit her tongue just in time to keep from telling Tate what Logan had said the last time he took her out to dinner. Like a child caught with her hand in the cookie jar, Abby flushed and lowered her gaze.

"Don't feel embarrassed. I like a woman who enjoys her food."

Abby's smile was wavering. Tate thought she was worried about the size of her order.

"You do volunteer work at the zoo?" Abby hoped that by directing the conversation away from herself she could put their time back on an even keel.

"I've always loved animals."

"I could tell just from the way you talked to the ducks and the squirrels," Abby inserted, recalling the first time she'd seen Tate.

He acknowledged her statement with a shake of his head. "Even as a child I would bring injured animals home and do what I could to make them well."

"Why didn't you become a veterinarian?"

Tate ignored the question. "The hardest part was setting them free once they were well. I might have been a veterinarian if things in my life had gone differently, but I'm good with cars, too."

"You're a mechanic?" Abby asked, already knowing the answer. The callused hands told her that her guess couldn't be too far off.

"I work at Bressler's Auto Repair."

"Sure. I know it. That's across the street from the Albertsons' store."

"That's it."

So it had been coincidence that Abby had seen Tate in the store.

"I've been working there since I was seventeen," Tate added. "Jack Bessler is thinking about retirement these days."

"What will happen to the shop?"

"I'm hoping to buy it," Tate said as he fingered his fork, nervously rotating it between two fingers.

It wasn't her imagination this time. Tate was uneasy. He paused and ran his fingers up and down the fork, not lifting his gaze from his silverware.

Their meal was as scrumptious as Abby knew it would be. Whatever was bothering Tate was soon gone and the remainder of the evening was spent talking, getting to know each other with an eagerness that was as strong as their mutual attraction. They talked nonstop for hours, sauntering lazily along the water's edge and laughing. Neither appeared eager to bring their time together to a close.

By the time Abby arrived home it was nearly midnight. She floated in the front door on a cloud of happiness. Even as she readied for bed, Abby couldn't forget how wonderful the night had been. Tate was a man she could talk to, really talk to. He listened to her and seemed to understand her feelings. Logan listened, but Abby had the impression that silently he was laughing at her. Maybe he wasn't, but that was what she felt. But perhaps that wasn't it at all. Maybe she was looking for things to soothe her conscience. Tate shared a part of himself with her, whereas Logan was the strong, silent type. That was fine, but after a year Abby sometimes believed she didn't know Logan.

The phone rang fifteen minutes after she was in the door.

Assuming it was Tate, Abby all but flew across the room to answer it. "Hello," she said in a low, sultry voice.

"Abby, is that you? You don't sound right. Are you sick?"

It was Logan.

Instantly, Abby stiffened and sank into the thick comfort of the chair. "Logan," she said in her normal voice. "Hi. Is something the matter?" He wouldn't be phoning this late otherwise.

"Not really."

"I suppose you've been waiting, I mean, I hope you haven't been trying long...I just got in...I mean..." she faltered as her thoughts tripped over each other, "but I thought you might be in bed," she finished lamely. He was obviously phoning to find out what time she got home.

Deftly Logan changed the subject to a matter of no importance, confirming Abby's suspicions. "No," he said stiffly, "I was just calling to see what time you wanted me to pick you up for class this week."

Of all the feeble excuses! Abby mused hotly. "Next time I go somewhere without you, do you want me to phone in so you'll know the precise minute I arrive home?" Abby asked crisply, fighting down her temper as her hand tightened around the telephone receiver.

His soft chuckle surprised her. "I guess I wasn't very original, was I?"

"No. This isn't like you, Logan. I've never thought of you as the jealous type."

"There's a lot you don't know about me," he answered on a wry note.

"I'm just beginning to realize that."

"Do you want me to pick you up for class this week, or have you made other arrangements?"

"Of course I want you to pick me up. I wouldn't want it any other way." Abby meant that. She liked Logan. The problem was she liked Tate, too.

Logan hesitated and the silence stretched between them. Abby was sure he could hear her racing heart over the telephone wire. But she hoped he couldn't read the confusion in her mind.

After work Monday afternoon, instead of heading back to her apartment and Dano, Abby stopped off at her parents' house.

"Hi, Mom." She sauntered into the kitchen and kissed her mother lightly across the cheek. "What's there to eat?" Hanging on the open refrigerator door, Abby surveyed the contents with interest.

"Abby," her mother admonished on a gentle note. "What's wrong?"

"Wrong?" Abby feigned ignorance.

"Abby, I'm your mother. I know you. The only time you show up in the middle of the week is if something is bothering you."

"Honestly, aren't I allowed an unexpected visit without parental analysis?"

"Did you and Logan get into a fight?" her mother persisted.

Glenna Carpenter's hair was as dark as Abby's richly colored chestnut hair, but Glenna's hair was streaked with gray, creating an unusual color a hairdresser's bottle couldn't reproduce. Glenna Carpenter was a young fifty-five, vivacious, outgoing and like Abby—a doer.

"What makes you say that? Logan and I never fight." Abby chewed off the end of a stalk of celery and closed the refrigerator. Taking the salt from the cupboard beside the stove she sprinkled a light coating across the remaining greens.

"Salt's rotten for your blood pressure." Glenna Carpenter took the shaker out of Abby's hand and replaced it in the cupboard. "Are you going to tell me what's wrong or do I have to torture it out of you?"

"Honest, Mom, there's nothing bugging me."

"Abby." Sapphire-blue eyes snapped with displeasure.

Abby couldn't restrain the soft laugh. Her mother had a way of saying more with one glare than some women did in a screaming tantrum.

Holding the celery with her teeth, Abby placed both hands on the counter and pulled herself up onto it, sitting beside the sink.

"Abby," her mother berated a second time.

"It's Logan," she said with a frustrated sigh. "He's become so possessive lately."

"Well, thank goodness. I'd have thought you'd be happy." Glenna's smiling eyes revealed her approval. "I was wondering how long it would take him."

"Mother." Abby wanted to cry. Deep within her heart, she'd known her mother would react like this. "It's too late—I've met someone else."

Glenna froze and a shocked look came over her face. "Who?"

"His name is Tate Harding."

"When?"

"A couple of weeks ago."

"How old is he?"

Abby wanted to laugh at her mother's questions. She sounded as if Abby were fifteen again and looking for permission to date. "He's twenty-seven and a hard-working respectable citizen. I don't know how to explain it, Mom, but I was instantly attracted to him. I think I'm falling in love."

"Falling in love," Glenna repeated, pouring herself a cup of coffee, her hand shaking as she lifted the mug to her mouth.

Abby knew her mother took her seriously when she drank coffee, which she usually reserved for mornings. A smile tugged at Abby's mouth, but she successfully kept it from quivering.

"I know what you must be thinking," Abby elaborated. "You don't even have to say it because I've already chided myself a thousand times. Logan's the greatest man in the world, but Tate is—"

"The ultimate?"

The suppressed smile formed dimples in Abby's cheeks. "Something like that."

"Does Logan know?"

"Of all the luck, they ran into one another at my apartment last week. It would have helped if they hadn't met like that."

"I think having Logan and Tate stumble into each other was more providential than you realize," Glenna murmured with infuriating calm. "I've always liked Logan. I think he's perfect for you."

"How can you say that?" Abby demanded indignantly. "We aren't anything alike. We don't even enjoy the same things. Logan can be such a stuffed shirt. You haven't even met Tate."

"No." Her mother ran the tip of one finger along the rim of her coffee cup. "To be honest, I never could understand why Logan puts up with you. I love you, Abby, you're my daughter; but I know your faults. Apparently Logan sees the same potential in you that I do."

"I can't believe my own mother would talk to me like this." Abby spoke to the ceiling, venting her irritation. "I come to her to pour out my heart and seek her advice and end up listening to a sermon."

Glenna laughed. "No sermon, I promise," she declared and dramatically crossed her heart. "Just some sound, motherly advice." An ardent light glowed from her eyes. "Logan loves you."

"Mother," Abby interrupted. "How can you say that? If he does, which I sincerely doubt, then he's never told me."

"No, I don't imagine he has. Logan is waiting."

"Waiting?" Abby was sarcastic. "For what? A blue moon?"

"No," Glenna returned sharply and took a long, deliberate sip of her coffee. "He's been waiting for you to grow up. As it is, you're impulsive, quick-tempered and immature."

Rarely had her mother spoken this candidly to her. Abby opened her mouth to deny the accusations, then closed it again. The words hurt, especially coming from her own mother, and she lowered her gaze to hide the onrush of emotional pain. Crystal tears hovered on the fringes of her long lashes.

"I'm not saying these things to hurt you," Glenna continued softly.

"I know that." A grimace revealed the dimples in Abby's cheeks. "You're right. I should be more honest, but I don't want to hurt Logan."

"Then tell him what you're feeling. To string him along would be unkind."

"But it's hard," Abby protested. "If I told him yesterday that I was going out with Tate he would have been angry. And miserable."

"And do you suppose he wasn't? I know Logan. If you said anything to him, he'd immediately step aside until you've settled things in your own mind."

"I know," Abby breathed in frustration. "But I'm not sure I want that either."

"You mean you want to have your cake and eat it, too," Glenna stated.

Abby resented the way her mother was looking at her. "I never have understood that saying."

"Then maybe you'd better think about it."

"In other words you're saying I should let Logan know how I feel about Tate."

"Yes."

The seriousness of her mother's look transferred itself to Abby. Confusion deepened her own brilliant blue eyes. She didn't want to hurt Logan, but she didn't want to lose him either.

"Today," her mother continued. "Now, before you change your mind."

Slowly Abby nodded her agreement. She hopped down from the counter with as much enthusiasm as a condemned man walking to the gallows.

"Thanks, Mom."

Glenna Carpenter gave Abby a motherly squeeze. "I'll be thinking about you."

"You'll like Tate."

"I'm sure I will. You always did have excellent taste." Abby's smile was tentative.

Directly from her mother's, Abby drove to Logan's accounting firm, which was situated half a block from her own office. His secretary recognized her name and buzzed Logan. Almost instantly the door to his office opened and Logan stepped into the outer office.

"Abby." He beamed her a warm smile. "What a pleasant surprise. Come in, won't you." He glanced over his shoulder and asked his secretary to hold his calls.

Abby took the leather chair opposite Logan's desk.

"To what do I owe this unexpected visit?"

"Logan." Abby's fingers had knotted into a tight fist in her lap. "Can we talk?"

He paused to look at his watch.

"It won't take long, I promise," she added hurriedly.

Leaning against the side of his desk, he crossed his arms in front of his chest. "What is it, Abby? I can't remember you looking this serious about anything."

"I think you have a right to know that I was with Tate Harding yesterday." Her heart was hammering so loudly Abby was convinced Logan must have heard it.

"Abby, you're as readable as a child. I was aware from the beginning who you were with," he explained firmly. "I only wish that you had been honest with me."

"Oh, Logan, I do apologize for that."

"It's forgotten."

How could he be so generous? So forgiving? She didn't deserve Logan Fletcher. Just when she was prepared to explain that she wanted to continue seeing Tate, Logan reached for her, drawing her into his embrace. As his mouth settled over hers, he drew from her a response so complete that Abby was left speechless and all the more confused. He kissed her as if he couldn't get enough of her sweet mouth, his lips plundering hers again and again.

"I've got a meeting in five minutes," Logan whispered against the side of her head as his fingers massaged her shoulders. "But believe me, holding you is far more tempting. Promise me you'll drop by the office more often. With that his mouth captured hers again in a kiss that melted Abby's defenses.

Chapter Three

Abby punched the pillow and determinedly shut her eyes. She shouldn't be having so much trouble falling asleep, she thought fighting back a loud yawn. Ten minutes later, she wearily raised one eyelid and glared at the clock radio. Two-thirty! Abby groaned audibly. Logan was responsible for this. He should have taken the time to listen to her. It would be a long time before she worked up the courage to talk to him about Tate a second time.

Tate had phoned after dinner and suggested an outing at the zoo for that weekend. Abby couldn't refuse him. Now she was paying the price; remorse and self-recriminations. Worse, it was all Logan's fault. It wasn't her problem that she hadn't been able to explain her feelings to Logan. She didn't mean to do anything behind his back. She liked both men, but the attraction she felt toward Tate was far more intense than the easy camaraderie she shared with Logan.

Bunching the feather pillow into a thick wad, Abby forced her eyes closed. She'd gone to Logan to explain that she wanted to date other men. She'd tried, really tried. There wasn't anything more that she could do.

When the radio went off at six, Abby wanted to scream. Sleep had been elusive the entire night. The few hours she'd managed to catch wouldn't be enough to see her through the day. Her eyes burned as she tossed aside the covers and sat on the edge of the mattress.

More from habit than from any sense of direction, Abby brushed her teeth and dressed. The tall glass of orange juice tasted like tomato, but she didn't open her eyes to investigate.

An hour later, Abby let herself into Dr. Robertson's office. Almost immediately the phone was ringing.

"Morning," Cheryl Hansen, the receptionist, smiled before answering the call.

Abby returned the friendly gesture with a weak movement of her mouth that only partially resembled a smile.

"You look like the morning after a wild and crazy night," Cheryl said as Abby hung her jacket in the room off the reception area.

"It was wild and crazy all right," Abby said after an exaggerated yawn. "But it's not what you think."

"Another late night with Logan?"

Abby's eyes widened. "No!"

"Tate then?"

"No. Unfortunately."

"I'm telling you, Ab, keeping track of your love life is getting more difficult all the time."

"I haven't got a love life," she murmured disgustedly and was unable to avoid yawning again. Placing the palm of her hand over her mouth as she yawned, Abby moved to the end of the long hallway.

The day didn't get any better. By noon, Abby recognized that there wasn't any way she was going to be able to attend tonight's class with Logan. One look at her troubled expression and he'd know immediately that she was deceiving him and seeing Tate again. And one thing she didn't need today was another confrontation with Logan. She didn't want to hurt him. But more than that—she didn't want to lie to him.

On her way back from lunch, Abby decided to phone his office. Her guilt grew heavier at the pleasure in his voice.

"Abby, this is a surprise."

"Hi, Logan." She groaned inwardly, hating herself all the more. "I hope you don't mind me phoning you like this."

"Not at all."

"I'm not feeling well." She paused, her hand tightening around the receiver. "I was thinking that maybe it'd be best if I skipped class tonight."

"What's wrong?" His genuine concern was nearly her undoing.

"Nothing, really. But I think I might be coming down with something." Like a terminal case of cowardice, her mind shot back.

"Have you seen a doctor?"

"It isn't necessary. Not yet. But I thought I'd stay home tonight and go to bed early," Abby mumbled, feeling more wretched every second.

"Do you need me to do anything for you?" The velvety texture of his voice was laced with sweet gentleness.

"No," she assured him quickly. "I'm fine. Really. I just thought I'd nip this thing in the bud and take it easy. If you don't mind, that is."

"Of course not. But promise me that if you need anything, you'll call."

"Oh, sure."

Abby felt even worse after making the phone call. By the time she returned to her apartment late that afternoon her excuse for not attending classes was more than real. Her head was throbbing unmercifully; her throat felt dry and scratchy and her stomach was queasy.

With her fingertips pressing against her temple, Abby located the aspirin in the kitchen cupboard and downed two tablets. Afterward she lay on the sofa, propped her head up with a soft pillow and closed her eyes. The phone rang and she sat up with a start. Dear Lord, don't let that be Logan, she prayed.

"Hello." Her reluctant voice was barely above a whisper.

"Abby, is that you?"

Immediately Abby breathed easier. It was her mother.

"Hi, Mom."

"What's wrong?"

"Nothing much. I've got a miserable headache."

"What's bothering you?"

"What makes you think anything's bothering me?" Her mother displayed none of the sympathy Logan had.

"Abby, I'm your mother. I know you. When you get a headache it's because something's troubling you."

Breathing in deeply, Abby glanced at the ceiling with rounded eyes. Sometimes her mother knew her better than she did herself.

"Did you talk to Logan yesterday?" Her mother continued the interrogation.

"Only for a little bit. He was on his way to a meeting."

"Did you tell him you want to continue seeing Tate?"

"I didn't get the chance," Abby shot back more aggressively than she'd intended. "Mom, I tried, but he didn't have the time to listen. Then Tate phoned me and asked me out this weekend and it sounded like so much fun. I didn't want to turn him down."

"So you're going out with Tate?"

"Logan doesn't know." Abby mumbled and exhaled miserably.

"And you've got a whopper of a headache?"

"Yes." The one word trembled from her lips.

"Abby," her mother's voice took on the serious note Abby knew all too well, "you've got to talk to Logan."

"I know."

"Your headache won't go away until you do."

"I know that too."

Dano strolled into the room and leaped onto the sofa, settling in Abby's lap. Grateful to have one friend left in the world, Abby stroked the cat with long, even strokes.

"Talk to Logan," Glenna Carpenter advised strongly.

"I will," Abby promised. For her own peace of mind, Abby decided, she'd have to.

It took her almost an hour to work up enough fortitude to dial Logan's number. His phone rang six times, and Abby sighed, feeling both angry and grateful that the inevitable had been postponed. As strongly as she was attracted to Tate, she didn't want to lose Logan. His ardent kiss yesterday had taken her by surprise. For a moment she'd had a fleeting glance at the way things could be between them. A tiny spark of passion had been ignited—one that flared bright with promise and then was quickly extinguished. But Abby had caught a glimpse of something she had never expected from Logan, and wasn't willing to sever their relationship entirely.

Yet at the same time she found Tate to be the most devastatingly wonderful man she'd ever known. He was everything she hoped to find: gentle, kind, fun.... But Logan could be all those things, too. More confused than ever, Abby rested her head against the back of the sofa cushion and closed her eyes.

The light knock on her door woke Abby an hour later. She sat up and rotated the stiff muscles of her neck. Dano remained on her lap and meowed angrily when she stood, forcing the cat to leap to the carpet.

"Yes," she called, before unlatching the safety chain.

"It's Logan."

Abby's hand was shaking visibly as she unlocked the door. "Hi," she said in a tight, high-pitched voice.

Logan stepped inside the apartment. "How are you feeling?"

"I don't know." She yawned, stretching her arms high above her head. "Fine, I guess." Her attention was drawn to a white sack Logan was holding. "What's that?"

A crooked smile slanted his mouth. "Chicken soup. I picked some up at the deli." He handed her the bag. "I want to make sure my best gal is well enough for the game tomorrow night."

Abby's head shot up. "Game? What game?"

"I wondered if you'd forgotten. We signed up a couple of weeks ago for the softball team."

This was the second summer they were playing in the office league. With her recent worries, softball had completely slipped Abby's mind. "Oh, *that* game." Abby wanted to scream with frustration. She'd never be able to avoid Logan. Too many activities linked them together—work, classes, and now softball.

She took the soup into the kitchen, removing the large plastic cup from the sack. The aroma of chicken and noodles wafted through the small kitchen. If Logan knew what was really wrong, he wouldn't put up with her—and she couldn't blame him.

He followed her into the cozy room and slipped his arms around her waist from behind. His chin rested on top of her head as he spoke. "I woke you, didn't I?"

She nodded, resisting the urge to turn and slip her arms around his waist and bury her face in his chest. "But it's probably a good thing you did. I would have gotten a crick in my neck sleeping on the couch with Dano on my lap."

Logan's breath stirred the hair at the top of her head. The secure feel of his arms holding her close was enough to cause tears to burn at the back of her eyes.

"Logan," she breathed his name in a husky murmur, "why are you so good to me?"

He turned her so that she couldn't avoid his eyes. Unable to look him directly in the eye, she concentrated her gaze on the small cleft in his chin. Nervously Abby moistened her lips with the tip of her tongue.

"I would have thought you'd have figured it out by now," he said as he slowly lowered his mouth to hers.

A sweetness flooded Abby at the tender possession of his mouth. She wanted to cry and beg him not to love her. Not yet. Not until she was sure of her feelings. But the gentle caress of his lips prevented the words from ever forming. Of their own volition, her hands moved up his shirt and over his shoulders, reveling in the smooth feel of his strength.

His hands, at the small of her back, arched her closer as he inhaled deeply. "I've got to go or I'll be late for class. Will you be all right?"

Speaking was impossible and it was almost more than Abby could do to simply nod her head.

He straightened slightly, relaxing his grip. "Take care of yourself." With an infinite gentleness he brushed the hair from the sides of her face. His eyes smiled lovingly into hers.

Again it was all Abby could do to simply nod.

"I'll pick you up tomorrow at six-thirty. If you're up to it, we can grab a bite to eat after the game."

"Okay." Even to herself the word sounded unnaturally high.

Logan paused and studied her for a moment. "You're sure you'll be all right?"

"I'll be fine," she managed shakily and walked him to the door. "Thanks for the soup."

He paused and ran one finger along her chin. "I've got to take care of the team's first baseman, don't I?" His mouth brushed hers and he was gone.

Leaning against the door, Abby looked around her grimly. If she felt uneasy before, now she felt wretched.

Shoving the baseball cap down on her long brown hair, Abby couldn't restrain a sense of excitement. She did enjoy softball. And Logan was right—she was the best first baseman the team was likely to find. Not to mention her hitting ability. For a long time Abby assumed Logan played because he knew how much she enjoyed the game and the competition. He wasn't much of a player himself. Only after they'd played a few times did she recognize that Logan apparently enjoyed himself as much as she. He just didn't have the competitive edge she did. More than once Logan was responsible for an error. But no one seemed to mind and Abby didn't let it bother her.

As usual he was punctual. "Hi. I can see you're feeling better."

"Much better." Her gaze skidded across his light-blue slacks and plaid sports shirt. "Logan," she breathed, "don't you have any jeans?"

He looked surprised for a minute. "No. Should I?"

Abby shrugged. "I don't know. I thought everyone wore washed-out jeans and sweatshirts." She glanced down over her own faded jeans and her ten-year-old T-shirt. It was silly to let what he wore to a softball game bother her. "Here." She handed him four sticks of gum.

"What's this?"

"Gum. It's to chew during the game."

"I know what it is," he murmured and breathed out irritably. "I'm asking you why you're giving it to me."

Impatiently, Abby clenched and unclenched her fists. "Logan, if you knew the first thing about baseball you'd realize that the players chew either tobacco or gum. Sometimes both."

"I don't."

Abby shifted the wad of bubble gum to the other side of her mouth. "It could help your game."

"Gum isn't going to make me a better hitter."

Abby wanted to scream with frustration.

"Abby," he murmured irritably. "I have a feeling this is another one of those driving-to-Des Moines-and-back ideas of yours. I am who I am. If you want to chew gum and be a 'real' softball player, feel free—but don't force it on me."

Without another word, Abby took her freshly oiled mitt and tucked her keys into her hip pocket after locking the apartment door. A purse would only get in the way at the game.

"I thought 'real' women carried purses," Logan said and gave her that lazy, crooked smile of his.

For an instant Abby's blue eyes sparked until she saw the humor in his observation. "Touché, Logan," she said with a good-natured smile. "Touché."

The game was scheduled to be played in Diamond Lake Park, and Abby was half-afraid Tate would stumble into them. She wasn't sure how often he ventured into the park and . . . She put a bridle on her worries. Heavens, she was getting paranoid.

Most of the team had arrived by the time Abby and Logan sauntered onto the field. The Jack and Jill Softball League was recreational. Of all the team members, Abby was the one who tended to take the game most seriously. The team positions were alternated between men and women. Since Abby played first base, a man was at second. Logan was in the outfield.

The team they were playing was from a local church that Abby remembered having beaten last summer.

Dick Snyder was their office team's coach and strategist. "Hope that arm's as good as last year," Dick said to Abby, who beamed him a brilliant smile. It was gratifying to be appreciated.

After a minimum of warm-up exercises and a few practice pitches their team left the field. Logan was up at bat first. Abby cringed at the stiff way he held himself.

"Logan," she shouted encouragingly, "flex your knees."

He did as she suggested and swung at the next pitch. The ground ball skidded past the shortstop and Logan was safe on first.

Abby breathed easier and gave him a triumphant smile.

Patty Martin got up to bat second. Abby took one look at the shy, mousy girl and knew she would constitute an immediate out.

"Come on, Patty," Abby called out, hoping to give the girl some self-confidence, "you can do it."

The girl held the bat up awkwardly and bit into her bottom lip as she glared straight ahead at the pitcher. She swung at the first three balls and missed each one.

Dick pulled Patty aside and gave her a pep talk before she took her place on the bench.

Abby scooted over to Patty afterward and patted her knee. "I'm glad you decided to play with us." She meant that honestly. From the looks of her, Patty could do with some friends.

"But I'm terrible." Patty's gaze was centered on her clenched hands and Abby noticed how white her knuckles were.

"You'll get better," Abby said with more confidence than she felt. "Everyone has to learn, and believe me, every one of us makes outs. Don't worry about it."

By the time Abby was up to bat, there were two outs and Logan was still at first. Her standup double and a home run by the hitter following her made the score 3-0.

The count remained the same until the bottom of the eighth. Logan was playing the outfield when a high fly ball went over his head.

Frantically jumping up and down at first base, Abby screamed, "Throw the ball to second. Second." She watched in horror as Logan turned and faced the third baseman. "Second!" she yelled angrily.

The third baseman missed the catch and the batter went on to home, giving his team their first run.

Abby threw her glove down and, with her hands placed defiantly on her hips, stormed onto the outfield and up to Logan. "I told you to throw the ball to second."

He gave her a mildly sheepish look. "Honestly, Abby, with all that gum in your mouth I couldn't hear what you were saying."

Groaning, Abby slapped her palms against the sides of her jeans and returned to her position.

They won the game 3-1 and gathered afterward at a local pizza parlor.

"You're really good," Patty admitted, sitting beside Abby.

"Thanks," she said and smiled into her soft drink. "I was on the high-school team for three years, so I had lots of practice."

"I don't know that I'll ever learn."

"Sure you will," Logan inserted. "Besides, we need you. Didn't you notice that we'd be short one woman if it wasn't for you?"

Abby hadn't noticed that, but was pleased that Logan brought it up. This quality to make people feel wanted and liked was the very one that had drawn Abby to Logan on their first date. He'd never win a Mr. Universe competition, but he was kind and gentle-hearted.

"I know I'm awful, but I really like playing. It gives me a chance to know all of you better," Patty added shyly.

"We like having you," Abby confirmed. Patty seemed to want the reassurance that she was needed and appreciated, and Abby didn't mind echoing Logan's words.

They ate their Italian-sausage pizzas and joked while making plans for the game the following Wednesday evening.

Dick Snyder and his wife gave Patty a ride home. Patty hesitated in the parking lot. "Goodbye, Logan," she said timidly. "I'll see you soon."

Abby smiled secretly to herself. Patty was attracted to Logan. The girl had praised his skill several times during the evening. Abby didn't blame Patty. Logan was wonderful. True, he wasn't Reggie Jackson on the baseball field. But he'd made it to base every time he was up at bat.

Logan dropped Abby off at her apartment, but didn't accept her invitation to come in for a glass of iced tea. To be honest, Abby was grateful. She didn't know how much longer she could hide from Logan the fact she was continuing to see Tate. And she refused to lie if he asked her.

The remainder of the week went relatively smoothly. She didn't talk to Logan, which made things easier. Abby realized that Sunday afternoon with Logan would be difficult after spending Saturday with Tate, but she decided to worry about it then.

She woke Saturday morning with a sense of expectancy. Tate was meeting her in the park after she finished tutoring Mai-Ling and from there they were going to drive out to Apple Valley and the Minnesota Zoo where he did volunteer work.

She dressed in her best linen summer dress and weaved her long brown hair into a French braid. A glance in the mirror revealed that she looked her best.

Mai-Ling met her and nodded knowingly. "You and Tate seeing each other today?"

"We're going to the zoo."

"The animal place, right?"

"Right."

Abby's attention drifted while Mai-Ling did her lesson. The woman's ability was increasing with every meeting. Judging from the work Mai-Ling brought for Abby to examine, the young woman wouldn't be needing her much longer.

The pair had finished the lesson and were laughing when Abby looked up and noticed Tate sauntering across the lawn toward her.

Again she was struck by the sight of this ruggedly appealing male. He was dressed in jeans, a short-sleeved shirt and cowboy boots.

His rich brown eyes seemed to burn into hers. "Hello, Abby." He greeted Mai-Ling, but his eyes left Abby's only for a second.

"I'll catch my bus," said Mai-Ling, excusing herself, but Abby barely noticed.

"You're looking especially beautiful today," Tate commented, taking her hand in his.

A tingling sensation scooted up her arm at his touch. Her nerves felt taut and raw just from standing beside him. Abby couldn't help wondering what it would be like if Tate kissed her. Probably the closest thing to heaven this side of earth.

"You look deep in thought."

Abby smiled up at him. "Sorry. I guess I was."

They chatted easily as Tate drove toward Apple Valley. Abby learned that he'd been a volunteer for three years, working as many as two days a week at the zoo.

"What animals do you care for?" Abby's curiosity was piqued.

Tate answered her without taking his eyes from the road. "Most recently I've been training a llama, but I also do a lot of work with the birds. In fact, I was recently asked to assist in the bird show."

"Will you?" Abby remembered seeing Tate that first day with the ducks and how naturally he interacted with them.

"Probably."

"What other kinds of things do you do?"

Tate's returning smile was short-lived. "Nothing all that glamorous. I help at feeding time and clean the cages. Sometimes I groom and exercise the animals."

"What are you doing with the llama?"

"Mostly I've been helping to familiarize him with people. We'd like Larry to join his brother in giving children rides."

Abby couldn't picture anyone on the back of the long-necked South American animal, but didn't say so.

Tate parked the car and, with an economy of movement, came around to her side and opened the passenger door, helping her out. He kept her hand tucked in his as he led the way to the entrance.

"You love it here, don't you?" Abby asked as they cleared the gates.

"I do. The zoo gives us a rare opportunity to discover nature and our relationship to other living things." A glint of laughter flashed briefly from his eyes as he turned toward her. "I didn't know I could be so profound."

Someone called out to Tate, and Abby watched him respond with a brief wave.

"Where would you like to start?"

The zoo was divided into five regions and Abby chose Tropics Trail, an indoor oasis of plants and animals from Asia.

"There are more than 650 animals housed in here," Tate explained, "and about 15,000 plants."

Abby was astonished. During her lifetime she'd been to the zoo several times, but she'd never had such an apt guide as they took an extended tour.

Three hours later, they gave their feet a rest and sat in the zoo theater. The multi-image slide show fascinated Abby.

"Promise you'll bring me again." Abby's eyes were held by Tate's with mesmerizing ease.

"I promise," he whispered as he led her toward his car.

Just the way he said it made her feel weak at the knees. Tate was special, more special than any man she'd ever known. Logan was wonderful, too. Any woman would consider herself fortunate to find two men she could care for so deeply.

Tate drove back to Minneapolis and stopped at a Mexican restaurant as they neared Diamond Lake Park. Abby had passed it on several occasions but had never eaten there.

A young Hispanic girl smiled at them and, with two menus tucked under her arm, led them to a table.

Tate spoke to the woman in Spanish. The girl nodded her head and turned around.

"What did you ask?" Abby whispered the question.

"I wanted to know if we could eat outside. You don't mind, do you? The evening is lovely."

"No, that sounds great." But she did care. Immediately the thought flashed through her mind that Logan might drive past and see her there eating with Tate. Abby managed to squelch her worries as she opened the menu and studied its contents. But her appetite had unexpectedly disappeared.

"You've got that thoughtful look again," Tate remarked after they'd been seated and handed the menus. "Is everything okay, Abby?"

"Oh, sure," she responded quickly and offered him a bright smile.

Abby decided early what she'd order and took the opportunity to study Tate as he reviewed the menu. His brow was creased in heavy lines, his eyes narrowed in concentration. When he happened to glance up and find her looking at him he quickly set the menu aside.

An awkwardness followed. It continued until the waitress finally stopped at their table. Abby ordered cheese enchiladas and Tate echoed her choice. "I had a good day today," Abby said in an attempt to breach the silence after the waitress left.

"I did too." Tate sounded stiff, as if he were suddenly uneasy.

"Is something the matter?" Abby asked after a time.

An electric silence filled the air. It could have been Abby's imagination, but it looked as if Tate was struggling within himself and ill at ease.

"Tate?" she prompted.

He leaned forward and pinched the bridge of his nose before exhaling. "No...nothing."

Long after Tate dropped her off at the apartment, Abby couldn't shake the sensation that something was greatly troubling him. Twice after they'd eaten he seemed about to say something, but both times stopped himself.

Abby's thoughts were heavy as she drifted into sleep. Tomorrow she would be seeing Logan. She had to tell him that she'd decided to date Tate; delaying it any longer was a grave disservice to them both.

Sunday afternoon, Logan sat on the sofa beside Abby and reached for her hand. It was all she could do not to take it away. So often in the past Abby had wanted Logan to be more demonstrative. And now that he was, it caused such turmoil inside her that she wanted to cry.

"You're looking pale, Abby. Are you sure you're feeling all right?" he asked her, his voice gentle with concern.

"Logan, I've got to talk to you," she blurted out miserably. Her voice shook and Abby knew that if he responded with anger, she'd burst into tears.

"What you need is to get out of this stuffy apartment." He stood up bringing her with him. Tucking an arm around her trim waist, Logan directed her out of the apartment and across the street to his car.

Abby didn't have time to protest as he opened the door and helped her inside.

"Where are we going?" she asked, confused and miserable.

"For a drive."

"I don't want to go for a drive."

Logan diverted his gaze from the road long enough to narrow his eyes slightly on her. "Abby, what is it? You look like you're about to cry."

"I am." She swallowed convulsively and bit into her bottom lip. "I want to go back to the apartment."

Logan pulled over and cut the engine. "Abby, what's wrong?" he asked solicitously.

Abby climbed out of the passenger side and leaned against the side of the car. The blood was pounding wildly in her ears. Her arms hugged her waist.

"Abby?" he prompted softly as he joined her.

"It's your fault," she murmured unreasonably. "I tried to tell you on Monday. I even went to your office to talk to you, but you had some stupid meeting."

He didn't argue with her. "Is this about Tate?"

"Yes," she blurted. "I went to the zoo with him yesterday. All week I've felt guilty because I knew you don't want me to see anyone but you."

Abby chanced a look at Logan. He displayed no emotion. His eyes remained dark and unreadable as if they were discussing the weather or something of no concern to him. "Do you want to continue seeing him?"

"I like Tate. I've liked him from the moment we met in the park," Abby admitted in a low whisper. Her fingers ached from clenching together so tightly.

"And do you want to know him better?" His eyes seemed to draw her toward him like a magnet.

"Yes," she whispered, taking one hesitant step to his side.

"Then you should," he said evenly.

"Oh, Logan," she said with a giant rush of oxygen, "I was hoping you'd understand."

"I do, Abby." He stood and placed his hands deep within his pants pockets and walked toward the car and opened the passenger side for her.

"Where are you going?"

He looked mildly surprised. "I'm taking you home."

The smile that touched the corners of his mouth didn't reach his eyes. "Abby, if you're dating Tate, then you won't be seeing me."

Chapter Four

Abby's blue eyes widened and her voice trembled slightly with demand. "What do you mean?"

Logan turned toward her. His gaze had darkened and grown more intense. An almost imperceptible movement along the line of his jaw revealed a faint tightening. "How long have we been dating?" he asked, but his voice displayed nothing.

"Almost a year now. What's that got to do with anything?"

Logan ignored her question. "If you don't know how you feel about me in that time, then I can't see continuing a relationship."

Abby unclenched her fist, feeling the impotent anger swell within her. "You're trying to blackmail me, aren't you?"

"Blackmail you?" Logan snapped angrily. He paused and breathed in deeply. "No, Abby, that isn't my intention."

"But you're saying that if I go out with Tate, then I can't see you," she returned with a short, bitter laugh. "You're not being fair. I like you both. You're wonderful, Logan, but... but so is Tate."

"Then decide. Which one of us do you want?"

Logan made it sound so simple. "I can't," she inhaled a shaky breath and raked a weary hand through the long length of her hair. "It's not that easy."

"Do you want Tate and me to slug it out? Is that it? The winner takes the spoils?"

"No!" she cried, shocked and angry.

"You've got the wrong man if you think I'll do that."

Tears shimmered like brilliant sapphires in Abby's eyes. "That's not what I want, and you know it."

"Then what *do* you want?" The low question was harsh.

"Time. I need to sort through my feelings. When did it become a crime to be uncertain? I barely know Tate—"

"Time," Logan interrupted, but the anger in his tone wasn't directed at her. "That's exactly what I'm giving you. Take however long you need. When you've decided what you feel, let me know."

"But you won't see me?"

"Seeing you will be unavoidable. Our offices are half-a-block apart—in addition to the softball team."

"Classes?"

"No. There's no need for us to meet each other there."

Tilting her chin downward, Abby briefly closed her eyes against the rush of hurt. Logan could remove her from his life effortlessly. His apparent indifference pierced her heart.

Without a word Logan drove her back to the apartment and parked, but he didn't shut off the engine.

"Before you go," Abby said, her quivering voice as weak as a whisper, "would you hold me? Just once?"

Logan's hand tightened on the steering wheel until his knuckles were strained and white. "Do you want a comparison? Is that it?" he asked in a cold, stiff voice.

"No, that wasn't what I wanted." She reached for the door handle. "I'm sorry I asked."

Logan didn't move. They drew each breath in unison. Unflinching, their eyes held each other until Logan, his clenched jaw, hard and proud, became a watery blur and Abby lowered her gaze.

"Phone me, Abby. But only when you're sure." The words were meant as a dismissal and the minute she was out of the car, he drove away.

Abby's knees had felt so weak she sat down as soon as she was inside her apartment. She was stunned and hurt. She'd expected Logan to be angry, but she'd never expected this: that he wouldn't see her again. She had only tried to be fair. Hurting Logan, or Tate for that matter, was the last thing she wanted. But how could she be expected to know what she felt toward Tate? Everything was so new yet. They barely knew each other. He hadn't so much as kissed her. Abby had only wanted to be honest with them both. It wasn't right that Logan should treat her this way.

She moped around the house for a couple of hours and decided to pay her parents a visit. Her mother would be as shocked at Logan's reaction as she had been. Abby felt she needed to talk to her mother.

The short drive to her parents' house was accomplished in a matter of minutes. But the front door was locked and her parents appeared to be out. Belatedly, Abby recalled her mother saying something about going camping that weekend.

Abby sat on the front steps, unreasonably angry. Her mother's timing couldn't have been worse. Telling Logan that she was going to see Tate had been her mother's idea in the first place. And look where it had gotten her.

Never had a Sunday been so dull. Abby drove around for a time, picked up a hamburger at the drive-in and washed her car. The day without Logan seemed empty. This thought surprised Abby.

Lying in bed that night, Abby closed her eyes. If she had missed Logan, then he was certain to have felt that same sense of loss. This arrangement could work both ways. Logan would soon discover how empty his life was without her. The knowledge produced a small, contented smile.

The phone rang Monday evening and Abby glanced at it anxiously. It had to be Logan. One day. Logan couldn't make it one day without talking to her. A sense of triumph swelled within her as she picked up the receiver.

"Hello," she greeted cheerfully. She didn't want Logan to get the impression she was pining away for him.

"Abby, it's Tate."

Tate. An unreasonable rush of disappointment filled her. What was the matter with her? This whole mess was because she wanted to see more of Tate.

"How about a movie Friday evening?"

"I'd like that," she exhaled softly.

"You don't sound yourself. Is something wrong?"

"No," she denied quickly. "What movie would you like to see?"

They spoke for a few minutes longer and Abby managed successfully to steer the conversation from herself. For those few minutes, Tate helped her forget how miserable she was, but the sense of loss and frustration returned the moment she replaced the receiver.

Tuesday evening, Abby waited outside the community center hoping for the chance to see Logan before class. She planned to give him a regal stare that would reveal how content she was without him. Naturally if he gave a hint of how miserable he was, she might succumb and speak to him. But either he'd arrived before her or, he came after she'd gone inside the building, because Abby didn't catch a glimpse of him anywhere. Maybe he'd even skipped class, but she doubted that. Logan loved chess.

Calligraphy class remained a blurr in her mind as she hurried out the door to the café across the street. She'd met Logan there after class for weeks. He would come, Abby was convinced of it. Mentally, she pictured how their eyes would meet and intuitively they'd know that being apart like this was wrong for them. Their gaze holding, Logan would walk to her table, slip in beside her and take her hand. He might even raise it to his lips, but any outward display would be unnecessary. Everything would be there in his eyes for her to read.

The waitress gave Abby a surprised glance and asked if she was sitting alone tonight as she handed her the menu. Dejectedly Abby revealed that she was alone...at least for now.

When Logan entered the café, Abby straightened, her heart racing at double time. He looked great. But, she reminded herself, Logan wasn't one to display his emotions openly. Their eyes met and he gave her an abrupt nod before sliding into a booth on the opposite side of the room.

So much for daydreams, Abby mused angrily. Well fine, he could sit there all night, but she refused to budge. Logan would have to come to her. Determinedly she studied the menu, pretending indifference. When she couldn't stand it any longer, she chanced a look at him from the corner of her eye. He now shared his booth with two others and was chatting easily with his friends. Abby's heart sank.

"I'm telling you, Mother," Abby cried miserably the next afternoon in her mother's kitchen. "This whole thing's been blown out of proportion."

"What makes you say that?" Glenna Carpenter closed the oven door and set the meat loaf on top of the stove.

"Logan isn't even talking to me."

"It doesn't seem like there's been much opportunity. But I wouldn't worry. He will tonight at the game."

"What makes you so sure of that?" Abby swung her legs and leaped down from her position on the counter-top.

Glenna straightened and wiped her hands on her ever-present terry cloth apron. "Things have a way of working out for the best, Abby," she continued nonchalantly.

"Mom, you've been telling me that all my life and I've yet to see it happen."

Glenna chuckled and slowly shook her head. "It happens every day of our lives. Get your head out of the clouds, girl, and look around." Deftly she turned the meat loaf onto the platter. "By the way, didn't you say your game was at six o'clock?"

Abby nodded and glanced at her watch, surprised that the time had passed so quickly. "I've got to rush. Bye, Mom." She gave her mother a light peck on the cheek. "Wish me well."

"With Logan or the game?" Teasing blue eyes so like her own twinkled merrily.

"Both!" Abby laughed and was out the door.

Glenna followed Abby to the porch. Abby felt her mother's sober gaze following her as she hurried down the front steps and to her car. There was a brooding, thoughtful look about her mother she had witnessed only rarely. This thing with Logan was as worrisome to her as it was to Abby.

Almost everyone was on the field warming up when Abby arrived. Immediately her gaze sought out Logan. He was in the outfield pitching a ball to another of the men players. Abby successfully suppressed the rush of emotion she felt whip through her like a brushfire on a dry field. Who would have believed she'd feel so lost and unhappy without Logan? If he saw that Abby had arrived, he gave no indication.

"Hi, Abby," Patty called, and waved from the bench. She, too, had apparently just arrived.

Abby's returning smile was absent. "Hi."

"Wait until you see me bat." Patty beamed happily, pretending to swing at an imaginary pitch. Then placing her hand over her eyes as the fantasy ball flew into left field, she added: "I think I'll be up for an award by the end of the season."

"Good." Abby's gaze was preoccupied as she drank in the sight of Logan. He looked so good. So vital. Couldn't he have the decency to have lines at his eyes or a few gray hairs since she'd last seen him? He had to be suffering. She was, and that wasn't what she'd wanted or expected.

"Logan took me to see the Twins play Monday night and gave me a few pointers afterward," Patty continued speaking.

Abby couldn't believe what she was hearing. A few pointers, her mind shot back. I'll just bet he did! Logan and Patty?

Some of the shock must have shown in her eyes because Patty added hurriedly, "You don't mind do you? When Logan phoned, I asked him about the two of you and he said that you'd both decided to start seeing others."

"No," Abby returned flippantly, the anger building. "Why should I mind?"

"I . . . I just wanted to be sure."

If Patty thought she would get an award for baseball, Abby was sure someone should nominate her for an Oscar. By the end of the game her mouth hurt from her permanent smile. She laughed, cheered, joked, visited and gave the impression she hadn't a care in the world. At bat she was dynamite. Her hurt was readily transferred to her swing and she didn't hit anything less than a double and made two home runs.

Once Logan had patted her back affectionately to congratulate her, Abby had stiffened and shot him an angry glare. It had taken him only one day. One day to take out Patty. That hurt. It hurt more than anything she could remember.

"Abby?" Logan's dark brows quirked questioningly. "What's wrong?"

"Wrong?" Although she gave him a blank look, she realized her cheeks had become colorless. "What could possibly be wrong? By the way, Tate said to say hello. He wanted to be here tonight, but something came up unexpectedly." Put that in your hat and stuff it, Abby thought childishly.

She didn't speak to him again.

Gathering the equipment together after the game, Abby tried not to remember the way Patty positioned herself next to Logan on the bench during the game and how the girl made an excuse to be near Logan at every opportunity.

"You're coming for hamburgers, aren't you?" Dick asked Abby for the second time.

Abby wanted to go. The get-togethers after the game were often more fun than the game itself. But she couldn't bear the curious stares that were sure to follow when Logan sat next to Patty and paid the other girl attention.

"Not tonight," Abby responded, slowly raising her head to give Dick a look of false candor. "I've got other plans." Abby noticed the way Logan's mouth curved in a mirthless smile. He'd heard that and come to his own conclusions. Good!

Abby regretted her hasty refusal later. The apartment was hot and muggy. Even Dano, her temperamental cat, couldn't decide if he wanted in or out.

After a cool shower, Abby fixed a meal of scrambled eggs, toast and a chocolate bar. She wasn't the least bit hungry, but she preferred to stuff herself than to give Logan an excuse to think he was the reason she was losing weight.

Miserable and unhappy, Abby sat on the sofa and turned on the television. A rerun of an old situation comedy helped block out the picture of Patty in Logan's arms and Abby didn't doubt that Logan had kissed Patty. The bright, happy look in Patty's eyes had told her as much.

Uncrossing her legs, Abby released a bitter sigh. She shouldn't care if Logan kissed a hundred women. But she did. It bothered her immensely.

With the television blaring to drown out the echo of Patty telling her about the fun she'd had with Logan, Abby reached for the chocolate bar and peeled off the wrapper. The sweet flavor of chocolate wouldn't ease the uncomfortable feeling in her stomach. But Abby knew it wasn't chocolate she wanted—she wanted Logan. Feeling wretched again, she set the candy bar aside and leaned her head back, closing her eyes.

By Friday evening, Abby was convinced all the confused feelings she had about Logan could be summed up in one sentence: The grass is always greener on the other side of the fence. The idea of dating Tate had been appealing when she was seeing Logan steadily. It only stood to reason that the reverse was also true. At least that was what Abby told herself repeatedly as she dressed for her date with Tate.

With her long brown hair a gentle frame around her oval face, she applied a light coat of makeup. With a secret little smile she splashed on an extra dab of cologne. Tate wouldn't know what hit him! The summer dress was one of her best: a baby-blue, two-piece that could be dressed up or down, so that she was as comfortable wearing it to a movie as she would be to a formal dinner.

When Tate arrived, he had on a pair of cords and a cotton shirt, open at the neck. His eyes widened appreciatively.

"You're lovely," he said with affection and kissed her lightly on the cheek.

"Thank you." Abby couldn't restrain the taste of disappointment. He looked at her the way one would a sister and his kiss wasn't that of a lover or someone who intended to be a lover.

They joked easily as they waited in line for the latest Spielberg movie and Abby was struck by the easy camaraderie they shared. It didn't take her long to realize that their relationship wasn't hot and fiery, sparked by mutual attraction. Instead, it was friendly and warm, almost lacking in imagination.

Tate brought a huge bucket of popcorn, which they shared in the darkened theater. But Abby noted that Tate appeared restless, often shifting position, crossing and uncrossing his legs several times. Once, when he assumed she wasn't watching, he laid his head against the back of the seat and closed his eyes. Was Tate in pain? she wondered.

Abby's attention drifted from the movie. "Tate," she whispered. "What's wrong?"

He stiffened and shook his head. "Nothing. Why?"

Rather than go into a detailed rundown of his restlessness, she simply shook her head and pretended an interest in the screen.

When they'd finished the popcorn, Tate reached for her hand. But Abby noted that it felt cold and unnatural. If she didn't know better, she'd swear he was terribly nervous. But why? Abby couldn't imagine what possible reason Tate would have to be nervous around her.

The evening was warm when they emerged from the theater.

"Are you hungry?" Tate asked, taking her hand, and again, Abby was struck by how unnaturally cold it felt.

"For something cold and sinful," she answered with a teasing smile.

"Beer?"

"No," Abby laughed outright. "Ice cream."

Tate laughed, too, and hand in hand they strolled toward the downtown area where Tate assured her he knew of an old fashioned ice-cream parlor. The Swanson Parlor was decorated in pink: pink walls, pink chairs, pink linen tablecloths and pink waitresses. Abby was waiting for a waitress when one passed their table and blended in so perfectly with the decor that neither she nor Tate noticed until the woman had whisked past.

"I think there's a method to their madness," Tate whispered, examining the menu.

Abby decided quickly on the banana split and mentioned it to Tate.

"That does sound good. I'll have one, too."

Abby closed her menu and set it aside. This was the third time they'd gone for something to eat, and each time Tate ordered the same thing she did. He didn't look like the insecure type. But maybe she was being overly sensitive. It didn't make much difference, anyway.

The rapport they shared made conversation easy and lighthearted. But several times Abby noted that the laughter in Tate was forced. His gaze would grow intent and throw the conversation off stride.

"I love Minneapolis," Abby commented as they left the ice-cream parlor. "I couldn't imagine living any other place in the world."

"Me either," Tate commented. "Would you care for a late-evening stroll?"

"I've always liked to walk," Abby said and looped her hand in the crook of his elbow.

Tate paused and smiled, but again Abby noted the sober look in his eyes. "I was born in California," he began.

"What's it like there?" Abby had never visited the West Coast.

"I don't remember much. My family moved to New Mexico when I was six."

"Hot, I bet," Abby prompted.

"It's funny, the kind of things the mind brings back. I don't recall what the weather was like. But I remember my first-grade teacher, Miss Grimes. She was pretty and tall," Tate chuckled and patted Abby's hand. "But I suppose all teachers are tall to a six-year-old. We moved again the middle of that year."

"You seemed to have moved around quite a bit," Abby commented, wondering why Tate had started talking about himself so freely. They'd seen each other several times now, and although they shared conversation freely, she knew little about his personal life.

"We moved five times in as many years," Tate continued. "We had no choice, really. My dad had a hard time holding down a job, and every time he lost one we packed up and moved, seeking another start, another escape." Tate's face hardened into an impenetrable mask. "We came to Minneapolis when I was in the eighth grade."

"Did your father finally find his niche in life?" Abby sensed that Tate was revealing something that he rarely shared with anyone. She felt honored, but surprised. He didn't seem the type to divulge this pain-filled part of himself with someone he barely knew. Their relationship was promising in some ways and disappointing in others, yet, Tate was baring his soul to her. She couldn't understand his need to at this point in their relationship.

"No, Dad died before he ever found what he was looking for." There was no disguising the pain and anger in his announcement. "My feelings for my father are as confused now as they were then." He turned toward Abby, his look solemn. A glimmer of something she couldn't read showed in his dark brown eyes. "I hated him and I loved him."

"Did your life change after he was gone?" Abby's question was barely above a whisper, respecting the deep emotion in Tate's eyes.

"Yes and no. A couple of years later I dropped out of school and got a job as a mechanic. My dad had taught me a lot, enough to impress Jack Bessler to hire me."

"And you've been there ever since?"

His alert gaze ran over her face. His mouth quirked at one corner. "Ever since."

"You didn't graduate from high school then, did you?"

"No."

That sadness was back in his voice. "And you resent that?" Abby inquired softly.

"I may have for a time, but I never fit in a regular classroom. I guess in some ways I'm a lot like my dad. Restless, unhappy, insecure. But I'm much more content working at the garage than I ever was in any schoolroom."

"But you've worked there for years now." Abby contradicted his assessment of himself. "How can you say that you're restless?"

He didn't acknowledge her question. "There's a chance I could buy the business. Jack's ready to retire and wants out from under the worry."

"That's what you really want, isn't it, Tate?"

"The business is more than I ever thought I'd have in a lifetime."

"But something's stopping you?" Abby could sense this more from the way his body grew tense as he spoke than from what he said.

"Yes." The stark emotion in his voice startled her.

"Are you worried about not having graduated from high school? Because, Tate, you can now. There's a program at the community center where I take calligraphy classes. You can get what they call a G.E.D.—General Education Diploma; I think that's what it means—anyway, all you need to do is talk to a counselor and—''

"That's not it," Tate interrupted her harshly and ran a hand across his brow in a disconcerted movement.

"Then what is it?" Abby asked vehemently, her smile determined.

Tate hesitated until the air between them was electric, arcing in the muggy heat like a storm ready to explode.

"What's the point of this discussion? I don't understand." Abby's voice lost some of its indignation. One minute Tate was exposing a painful part of his past, and the next he was growling at her like a wounded bear. What was it with men? Something had been bothering Tate all evening. First he'd been restless and uneasy, then brooding and thoughtful, lastly angry. Nothing made sense anymore.

He hardly said a word to her when he dropped her off at her apartment an hour later.

For an intense moment, Abby was convinced he wasn't going to ask her out again.

"What about Sunday?" he said finally. "We can take a picnic."

"I suppose." After this evening, Abby wasn't sure. He didn't sound as if he wanted her company and Abby wasn't sure why he bothered to ask her out.

"Fine." His response was clipped, with barely restrained anger.

Again he gave her a modest kiss, more a light brushing of their mouths than any real kiss. The kind of exchange one would expect from a brother.

Abby leaned against the closed door of her apartment, not understanding why Tate bothered to take her out. It seemed apparent that his interest in her wasn't romantic. And for that matter, the bone-melting effect she'd experienced at their first meeting had long since gone. Tate was a handsome man, but he wasn't what she'd expected.

Maybe the grass wasn't so green after all.

After a restless Sunday morning, Abby decided that she'd take a walk in the park. Logan often did and she hoped to run into him. She'd make a point of letting it be known that their meeting was purely coincidence. They'd talk. Small talk. Somehow she'd let him know, casually of course, that things weren't working out as she'd planned. Maybe she'd hint that she missed his company. That should be enough to break the ice without either of them losing their pride. And that was what this thing boiled down to: pride.

The park was crowded by the time Abby arrived. Standing just inside the grounds, Abby scanned the plush lawns for him and released a grateful sigh to find that he was sitting on a park bench reading. To her relief, Patty wasn't with him.

Planning her strategy, Abby stuck her hands in her pockets and strolled down the paved lane, hoping to look as if she had come for a cool walk in the park. Their meeting would be by accident.

Content, Abby brushed the hair from her face and paused, watching Logan, surprised at the emotion that came just from studying him. He looked wonderful—serene and peaceful—but then he always did. Little in life would jar Logan. He was the Rock of Gibraltar. They'd been dating for almost a year and Abby hadn't had any idea that so much of her life was interwoven with Logan's. She'd taken him for granted until he was gone, and the empty space in her life had shocked her. She'd been stupid and insensitive. And heaven knew how difficult it was for her to admit that she'd been wrong.

For several minutes Abby did nothing but watch him, appreciating him. A soothing calm settled over her as her gaze focused on Logan's shoulders. They weren't nearly as broad or muscular as Tate's, but somehow it didn't matter. Not now, not when she was hurting, missing Logan and his friendship. Abby had been looking forward to Sunday all week and realized that Sundays had always been special days because they were spent with Logan. It was Logan she wanted, Logan she needed, and Abby hoped desperately that she wasn't too late.

For a long time, Abby did nothing but study him. After a while her determination to talk to him grew all the stronger. To hell with her pride—Logan had a right to know her feelings. He'd been patient with her far longer than she deserved. Her stomach felt tight and queasy with nerves. Just when she gathered up enough courage to approach him, Logan closed his book and stood up. Turning around he looked straight toward her and didn't bat an eyelash or hesitate. He glanced at his watch and idly walked down the concrete pathway until he was within calling distance. Abby's breath froze as he glanced her way, blinked and looked in the opposite direction. Abby couldn't believe that he would purposely avoid her and she doubted that he would have been able to see her standing off to the side as she was.

Just when she was ready to step forward, Logan stopped to chat with two older men playing checkers. From her position, Abby saw the men motion for Logan to sit down, which he did. Within minutes he was deep in conversation with them. The three were obviously good friends.

Abby loitered as long as she could. What seemed like an eternity passed and still Logan stayed to chat with the two elderly gentlemen.

Defeated, Abby realized she'd have to hurry or be late for the picnic with Tate. Silently she slipped from her viewing position and started across the grounds toward her apartment. When she glanced over her shoulder, she noted that Logan was alone and watching a pair of young lovers kissing while lying on the grass. A look of such intense pain crossed his face that it was all Abby could do not to run to his side. He dropped his head into his hands and hunched forward as if the heaviest burden in the world was weighing upon him.

A tightness grew in Abby's mouth and extended all the way down her throat until it was painful to breathe. Tears filled her eyes. Logan loved her and had loved her from the beginning. Carelessly she had tossed his love aside. Logan was the best thing that had ever happened to her. It had taken only a few days separation to realize that she loved him too.

Tears rolled down her face and Abby quickly brushed them aside. Logan wouldn't want her to know that she'd seen him. She'd stripped him of so much it wouldn't be right to take his pride. Today she'd tell Tate that she wouldn't be seeing him again. If that was all Logan wanted, it would be a small price to pay. She'd run back to his arms and never leave him again.

By the time she got back to her apartment, Tate was at her front door. They greeted each other and Tate told her of a special place he wanted to show her near Apple Valley.

Both seemed preoccupied as they drove. Abby helped him unload the picnic basket, her thoughts going at breakneck speed. She folded the tablecloth over a picnic table while Tate spread out a blanket under a shady tree. They hardly spoke.

"Abby."

"Tate."

They both began together.

"You first," Abby murmured and sat down, circling her knees with her arms so that her chin rested on top of her bent legs. Here it was a beautiful sunny day, and she was so miserable it was all she could do not to cry.

Tate remained standing, hands in his pockets as he paced. Again, something was obviously troubling him.

"Tate, what is it?" Abby prompted.

"I didn't know it would be so hard to tell you," he said wryly and shook his head forcefully. "I meant to explain weeks ago."

"Tate?" What was he talking about? He wasn't making any sense.

His intent gaze settled on her, then flickered to the ground. "I tried to tell you Friday night after the movie, but I couldn't force the words out." He ran a weary hand over his sorrow-filled eyes and fell to his knees at her side.

Abby reached for his hand and held it. His look was intense and tortured.

"Abby." He released a jagged breath. "*I can't read.* I'll pay you any amount if you'll teach me."

Chapter Five

In one brilliant flash everything about Tate fell into place. He hadn't been captivated by her charm and natural beauty. He'd overheard her teaching Mai-Ling to read and knew that she could help him. That was the reason he'd sought her out and cultivated a friendship. She could help him.

Small things became clear in her mind. No wonder Tate ordered the same thing she did in a restaurant. Naturally their date Friday night had been awkward. He'd been trying to tell her then. How could she have been so blind? So insensitive?

Even now his eyes studied her intently, awaiting her response. They glimmered intensely, filled with pride, insecurity and fear.

"Of course I'll teach you," she said reassuringly.

"I'll pay you anything you ask."

"Tate." Her grip on his hand tightened. "I wouldn't take anything. We're friends."

"But I can afford to pay you." He took a wad of bills from his pocket and breathed in slowly, glancing at the money in his hand.

Again Abby recognized how difficult admitting his inability to read had been. "Put that away," Abby stated calmly and patted his hand. "You won't be needing it."

Tate stuffed the bills into his shirt pocket and released a ragged breath. "You don't know how relieved I am to have finally explained."

"I don't think I could have been more obtuse," she said, still shocked at her own stupidity. "I'm amazed that you've gotten along as well as you have. I was completely fooled."

"I've become adept at this. I've played this game from the time I was in grade school."

"What happened?" Abby questioned softly.

A sadness stole into his eyes that left them narrowed and drew his thick brows into a tight line. "I suppose it's because of all those times I was pulled out of school so we could move," he stated unemotionally. "We left New Mexico in the middle of the first grade and I never finished the year. Because I was big for my age my mother put me into the second grade the following September. The teacher wanted to hold me back but we moved again. And again and again." A hardness infected his voice as he released the bitterness. "By the time I was in junior high and we'd moved to Minneapolis, I had devised a multitude of ways to disguise the fact I couldn't read. I was the class clown, the troublemaker, the boy who'd do anything to get out of going to school."

"Oh, Tate." Her heart swelled with compassion.

Sitting beside her, Tate rubbed his hand across his face and smiled sadly. "But the worst part was getting up enough courage to tell you."

"You've never told anyone, have you?"

"No. It was like admitting I have some horrible disease."

"You don't have any disease." She tried to reassure him and felt pathetically inadequate.

"When can we start? There's so much I want to learn. So much I want to read and know." He sounded eager, his gaze level and questioning.

"Is tomorrow too soon?" Abby asked.

"I'd say it's about twenty years too late," Tate said with a bittersweet sigh.

Tate dropped Abby back at her apartment two hours later. Tomorrow she'd call the World Literacy Movement and have them send out the forms for her to complete regarding Tate. He looked jubilant, excited. Telling her of his inability to read had probably been the most difficult thing he had ever done in his life. She understood how formidable his confession had seemed because now she had to humble herself and phone Logan. And that, although major to her, was a small thing in comparison.

Abby wasn't unhappy at Tate's confession. True, her pride was stung for a brief moment. But overall she was relieved. Tate was the kind of man who would always attract women's attention. For a brief time she had been caught up in the masculine appeal. And if it hadn't been for Tate, it could have been a lot longer before she recognized how fortunate she was to have Logan.

The thought of phoning him and admitting that she was wrong had been unthinkable only a week ago. Had it only been a week? In some ways it felt like a year.

Abby glanced at the ceiling and prayed that Logan would be home. There was so much stored in her heart that she wanted to tell him. Her hand trembled as she lifted the receiver and tried to form positive thoughts. Everything would work out. Abby knew it would. She wanted Logan back and hadn't recognized how badly until it came time to dial.

She was so nervous her fingers shook and her stomach churned until she was convinced she was going to be sick. Inhaling, Abby held her breath as the phone rang the first time. Her lungs refused to function. Abby tightly closed her eyes during the second ring.

"Hello."

Abby breathed.

"Logan, this is Abby."

"Abby?" He sounded shocked.

"Can we talk? I mean, I can call back if this is an inconvenient time."

"I'm on my way out the door. Would you like me to come over?"

"Yes." She was surprised at how composed she sounded. "That would be great." She replaced the phone and tilted her head toward the ceiling. "Thank you," she murmured gratefully.

Looking down, Abby realized how casually she was dressed. When Logan saw her again, she wanted to bowl him over with her natural beauty.

Racing into her room, she ripped the two-piece dress she'd worn Friday night off the hanger. One glance in the mirror confirmed that it wouldn't do. Carelessly, Abby tossed it across her bed. She tried on one outfit and then another. Never had she been more unsure about what she wanted to wear. Finally she chose a pair of lavender slacks and a white blouse with an eyelet collar.

Abby was frantically brushing her hair when the doorbell chimed. She gripped the edge of the sink and took in a deep breath. A smile cracked the tight line of her mouth as she set the brush aside and walked into the next room.

"Hello, Abby." Logan said as he stepped into the apartment.

Her first impulse was to throw her arms around him and weep. A tightness gripped her throat. Whatever poise she'd managed to gather was shaken and gone with one look.

"Hello, Logan. You look well." He looked better than she could ever remember: secure, calm, supportive. "Would you like to sit down?" She gestured weakly toward the chair. Her gaze was fixed on his shoulders as he walked across the room and took a seat in the armchair.

"And before you ask," he interjected sternly. "No, I don't want anything to drink. Sit down, Abby."

Meekly she complied, grateful because she didn't know how much longer her knees would support her.

"You wanted to talk?" The lines at the side of his mouth deepened, but he wasn't smiling.

"Yes." She laced her hands together so tightly she was sure the blood supply to her fingers had been impaired. "I was wrong." Now that the words were out, Abby experienced none of the calm she expected.

"It wasn't a question of my being right or your being wrong," Logan contradicted. "I'm not looking for an apology."

Abby's lips trembled and she bit into the bottom corner. "I know that. But I felt I owed you one."

"No." He stood and with one hand in his pocket paced the width of the carpet. "That's not what I wanted to hear. I told you to phone me when you were sure it was me you wanted to go out with and not Tate." His look rested on her, his expression hooded.

Abby stood, her gaze bounced away from him, and she was unable to meet his eyes. "I am sure," she breathed. "I know now that it's you I want."

His mouth quirked in what could have been a small smile, but he didn't acknowledge her confession.

"You have every right to be angry with me." She couldn't look at him, afraid of what she would see. If he were to reject her now, Abby thought she'd prefer to die. "I've missed you so much," she mumbled and her voice wobbled. Her cheeks flamed with color. Abby couldn't believe how difficult this was. Tears glistened in her eyes as she bowed her head.

"Abby." Logan's arms came around her shoulders, bringing her within the comforting circle of his arms. He lifted her chin and lovingly read her face, his gaze narrowed and thoughtful. "You're sure?"

The growing lump in her throat made speech impossible. She nodded, letting all the love in her eyes say the words.

"Oh, Abby," he breathed and claimed her lips with a hungry kiss that told her of the depth of his feelings during their short separation.

Slipping her arms around his neck, Abby felt him shudder with a longing he'd held in tight rein all these months. He buried his face in the dark waves of her hair and held her so tight it was difficult to breathe.

"I've been so wrong about so many things," she confessed, rubbing her hands up and down his spine, reveling in the muscular feel of him.

Lowering himself to the sofa, Logan pulled Abby onto his lap and held her. His warm breath was like a gentle caress as she wound her arms around his neck and kissed him, wanting to make up to him for all the pain she'd caused them both. The wild tempo of her pulse made clear thought impossible. Hungrily, his mouth devoured hers, crushing her upper torso to his hard chest. His hands roamed possessively over her, as though he couldn't get enough of her.

Logan dragged his mouth from her, his low groan telling her that he must stop now.

"You're sure?" he asked as if he wasn't able to believe that she was his.

Abby pressed her forehead against his shoulder and nodded. "Very sure. I was such a fool."

His arm held her securely in place. "Tell me more, I'm enjoying this."

Unable to resist, Abby kissed the side of his mouth. "I thought you would."

"I take it you missed me."

"I was miserable."

"Good!"

"Logan," she cried softly and playfully nipped at his ear with her teeth. "It wouldn't do you any harm to tell me how lonely you were."

"I wasn't," he said jokingly.

Involuntarily Abby stiffened and swallowed back the hurt. "I know. Patty mentioned that you'd taken her to the Twins game."

Logan's smile was faintly wry. "We went with several others."

"It hurt that you could see someone else so soon."

"Honey." His hold tightened around her waist, bringing her closer. "It wasn't like you're thinking."

"But you said you weren't lonely."

"How could I have been? I saw you Tuesday and then at the game Wednesday."

"I know, but—"

"Are we going to argue?"

"A thousand kisses might convince me," she teased and rested her head upon his shoulder.

"I haven't got the willpower to continue kissing you without thinking of other things," he murmured in her ear as his hand stroked her hair. "I love you, Abby. I've loved you from the first time I asked you out." His gaze rested on the shimmering moistness of her mouth, his breathing less controlled than it had been a moment before.

"Oh, Logan." Fresh tears misted her eyes. She wanted to tell him how much she cared for him, but he continued cutting off her words.

"One look at Tate and I knew there wasn't any way I could compete with him. He's everything I'll never be. Tall. Strikingly handsome. Suave. I don't blame you for being attracted to him."

Abby straightened so she could look at this man she loved. Her hands lovingly framed his face. "You're a thousand things Tate could never be."

"I know this has been hard on you."

"But I was so stupid," Abby inserted.

He kissed her lightly, his lips lingering over hers. "I can't help feeling grateful you won't be seeing him again."

Abby lowered her eyes. She would be seeing Tate, but not the way Logan meant.

A stillness filled the room. Logan knew. "Abby?"

She gave him a feeble smile.

"You aren't seeing Tate, are you?"

Frantically her mind raced down deep-grooved channels. She couldn't reveal Tate's problem to anyone. Not for the world would she embarrass him, not when admitting he couldn't read had been so difficult. No matter how much she wanted to explain, she couldn't.

"I'd like to explain," Abby replied, her voice trembling.

Logan stiffened and lightly pushed her from his lap. "I don't want explanations. All I want is the truth. Will you or will you not be seeing Tate?"

"Not romantically," she answered, as tactfully and truthfully as possible.

Immediately Logan's gaze hardened into dark steel. "What other explanation could there be?"

"I can't tell you that," she said forcefully and stood up.

"Of course you can." A muscle worked in his tightened jaw as he clenched his fists. "We're right back where we started, aren't we, Abby?"

"No." She felt like shouting and screaming at him for being so unreasonable. Surely he recognized how difficult it had been for her to phone him and admit she was wrong?

"Will you stop seeing Tate, then?" he challenged.

"I can't." Her voice cracked with the desperate appeal for him to understand. "We live in the same neighborhood..." she murmured, stalling for time as her mind raced for an excuse. "I'll probably run into him... I mean, it'd be only natural, being that he's so close and all."

"Abby," Logan groaned impatiently. "That's not what I mean and you know it. Will you or will you not be *seeing* Tate?"

She hesitated, wavering in indecision. Knowing what it was doing to her relationship with Logan, Tate would want him to know. But she couldn't say anything without first clearing it with Tate.

"Abby?"

"I'll be seeing him, but please understand that it's not the way you assume."

For an instant, Abby saw the pain flash in Logan's eyes. The pain she witnessed was the same tormenting ache she was experiencing.

They stood with only a few feet separating them and yet Abby felt they had never been farther apart. Whole worlds seemed to loom between them. Logan's ego was at stake and his male pride was too fragile to allow her to continue seeing Tate, no matter what the reason.

"You won't stop seeing him," Logan challenged.

"I can't," Abby cried, just as angry.

"Then there's nothing left to say."

"Yes," Abby said forcefully, "there is, but you're in no mood to hear it. Just remember that sometimes things are not always as they appear."

"Goodbye, Abby," he answered without so much as hesitating. "And next time don't trouble me unless—"

Abby stalked across the room and threw open the door. "Next time I won't phone you," she said with a flippant cutting edge.

Reaction set in the minute the door slammed. Abby was so angry that pacing the floor did little to relieve the building anger. He couldn't say he loved her in one breath and turn around and storm out on her in another. Yet, Logan had done exactly that.

Once the anger dissipated, Abby began to tremble and felt the tears burning for release at the back of her eyes. Pride demanded that she forestall them. She wouldn't allow Logan to reduce her to that level. She shook her head and kept her chin raised. She wouldn't cry, she wouldn't cry, her mind repeated over and over as one tear after another slid down her cheeks.

"Who did you say was responsible for the literacy movement?" Tate asked, leafing respectfully through the first book.

"Dr. Frank Laubach. He was a missionary to the Philippine Islands in the 1920's. At that time the island people didn't have a written language. He gave them the written word and later invented a method of teaching adults to read."

"Is he alive now?"

Abby had greatly admired the man herself and knew what Tate was thinking. "No, he died in 1970, but not before his work had spread to 105 countries and 313 languages."

Tate continued leafing through the pages of the primary-level workbook. Abby wanted to start him at the most fundamental skill level, knowing his progress would be rapid. And at this point of his study, Tate would need all the encouragement he could get and the quick speed with which he completed the lower-level books was sure to help.

Abby hadn't underestimated Tate's enthusiasm. By the end of the first lesson he had relearned the alphabet and was reading simple phrases. Proudly he took the book home with him.

"Can we meet again tomorrow?" he wanted to know, standing just inside her apartment door.

"I've got classes tomorrow evening," Abby explained, "but if you like, we could meet for a half hour before—or after if you prefer."

"Before, I think."

The following afternoon, Tate showed up an hour early and seemed disappointed that Abby would also be occupied with softball Wednesday evening.

"It's an early game. We could get together afterward if you want."

Affectionately, Tate kissed her lightly on the cheek. "I want."

Again she noted that his fondness for her was more like that of a brother, or that of a pupil for a teacher. She was grateful for that, at least. He was wonderful to her. He continually brought her small gifts as a way of showing his appreciation. The gifts weren't necessary, but it salvaged Tate's pride and that was something she was learning more about every day—male pride.

Abby was dressing for the game Wednesday evening when the phone rang. She glanced at it wryly. No longer did she hold the wish that it would be Logan. He'd made his position more than clear.

"Hello."

"Abby, I've been worried about you."

"Hi, Mom." She forced some enthusiasm into her voice.

"Oh dear, it's worse than I thought."

"What's worse?"

"You and Logan."

"There is no more Logan and me," she returned forcefully.

A strained silence followed. "But I thought—"

"Listen, Mom," Abby cut in, unwilling to listen to her mother's postmortem. "I've got a game tonight. Can I call you back later?"

"Why don't you come over for dinner?"

"Not tonight." Abby hated to turn down her mother's invitation, but when she was this miserable she'd prefer not to see anyone.

"It's your birthday Friday," Glenna reminded her.

"I'll come for dinner then," Abby said with a feeble smile. Her birthday was only a few days away, she mused sadly, and she wasn't in any mood to celebrate. "But only if you promise to cook my favorite dish."

"Barbecued chicken!" her mother shot back, already thinking ahead. "It's as good as done."

"And, Mom," Abby continued, "you were right about Logan."

"What was I right about?" her mother questioned, her voice lifting slightly.

"He does love me, more than I thought possible, and I love him."

Abby thought she heard a small, happy sound.

"What made you realize that?" her mother questioned further.

"A lot of things," Abby stated noncommittally, "but mostly I realized that loving someone doesn't make everything perfect. I wish it did."

"I have the feeling there's a lot you're not telling me, Abby," Glenna said on a note of puzzled sadness. "But I know you well enough to realize that you will in your own good time."

Abby could deny none of her mother's observation. "I'll be at your place around six on Friday," Abby murmured. "And thanks, Mom."

"What are mothers for?" Glenna teased affectionately.

The disconnected phone line droned in Abby's ear before she realized she continued to hold the receiver. Trapped in the tangled web of her thoughts, Abby was surprised to notice that it was time to head for the park and the softball game. For the first time that she could remember, she didn't feel psyched up for the game. She wasn't sure she wanted to see Logan. It would be more

You know the thrill of escaping to a world of **EXOTIC LOCATIONS... EXCITING ADVENTURE... and ENDURING LOVE...**

Escape again...with 4 FREE novels and

Get a Folding Umbrella & Mystery Gift Free!

EVERY BOOK YOU RECEIVE WILL BE A BRAND-NEW FULL-LENGTH NOVEL!

Escape with 4 Silhouette Romance novels (a $7.80 Value) and get a Folding Umbrella & Mystery Gift Free!

painful than reassuring. And if he was to pay Patty special attention, Abby didn't know how she'd handle that. But Logan, after proclaiming his love, wouldn't do anything to hurt her. At least she knew him well enough to realize that.

The first thing Abby noticed as she walked onto the diamond was that Patty Martin had cut and styled her hair. The transformation from the straight mousy-brown hair to the short, bouncy curls was astonishing. The young girl positively glowed.

"What do you think?" Patty questioned in a tight hurried voice. "Your hair is always so pretty and..." She let the rest of what she was going to say fade.

Abby stiffened and held herself motionless. Patty had made herself more attractive for Logan. The girl desperately wanted Logan's attention and for all Abby knew, Patty was getting it. "I think you look great," Abby commented, unable to deny the truth.

"I was scared out of my wits," Patty admitted shyly. "It's been a long time since I was at the hairdresser's."

"Hey, Patty, they're waiting for you on the field," the team's coach and fellow player hollered.

"Right away, Dick," she called back happily, her eyes shining. "I've gotta go. We'll talk later, okay?"

"Fine." Softening her stiff mitt against her hand with unnecessary force, Abby ran to her position at first base.

Logan was practicing in the outfield.

"Abby," he called, and when she turned, she found his gaze level and unwavering. "Catch."

Nothing appeared to affect him. They'd suffered through the worst four days of their relationship and he looked at her as coolly and unemotionally as he would a dish of potato salad. She wanted to scream at him, but instead caught the softball and pitched it to the second baseman.

The warm-up period lasted several minutes. Abby couldn't recall a time she'd felt less like playing, and it showed.

"What's the matter, Ab?" Dick asked her at the bottom of the fifth inning after she struck out for the third time. "You're not your old self tonight."

"I'm sorry," she said as a frustrated sigh broke from her slightly parted lips. Her eyes didn't meet his level gaze. "This isn't one of my better nights."

"She's got other things on her mind." Logan's voice spoke from behind her, signaling that he was sitting in the bleachers one row above her. "Her boyfriend just showed up, so she'll do better."

Abby whirled around to face Logan. "What do you mean by that remark?"

Logan quirked his head in the direction of the parking lot. Abby's gaze followed his action and she wanted to groan aloud. Tate was walking toward the stands, hands in his pockets.

"Tate isn't my boyfriend," Abby's voice was thick with impatience.

"I suppose the terminology is passé in today's vernacular," Logan returned with mocking emphasis.

Stunned at the bitterness in him, Abby found no words to respond. They were both hurting, and in their pain they were lashing out at each other.

Logan slid from the bleachers for his turn at bat. Abby focused her attention on him, deciding she didn't want to make a fuss over Tate's unexpected arrival.

Logan swung wildly at the first pitch, hitting the softball with the tip of his bat. Abby could hear the wood crack as the ball went flying over the fence for a home run. Logan looked as shocked as Abby. He tossed the bat aside and ran around the bases to the shouts and cheers of his teammates. Abby couldn't remember Logan ever getting more than a single.

"Hi." Tate slid into the row of seats behind her.

"You don't mind if I come and watch, do you?" Tate asked as he leaned forward with a lazy grace.

"Not at all," Abby said blandly. It didn't make any difference now. She stared at her laced fingers, attempting to fight off the depression that seemed to have settled over her like a thundercloud. She was so caught up in her own sorrows that she didn't see the accident. Only the startled cries of those around her alerted her to the fact that something had happened.

"What's wrong?" Abby asked frantically as the bench cleared. Everyone was running toward Patty, who was clenching her arm and doubled over in agonizing pain.

Logan's clear voice could be heard above the confusion. "Stand back. Give her room." Gently he aided Patty into a sitting position.

Even to Abby's untrained eye it was obvious that Patty's arm was broken. Logan tore off his shirt and tied it around her upper body to support the injured arm.

The words "hospital" and "doctor" were flying around, but everyone seemed stunned and no one moved. Again it was Logan who helped Patty to her feet and led her toward his car in the parking lot. His calm, decisive actions imparted confidence to both teams. Only minutes before, Abby had been angry because he displayed so little emotion.

"What happened?" Abby asked Dick as they walked off the field.

"I'm not exactly sure." Dick looked a little shaken himself. "Patty was trying to steal a base and collided with the second baseman. When she fell, she put out her arm to catch herself and it twisted under her.''

"Will she be all right?''

"Logan seemed to think so. He's taking her to the emergency room. He said he'd let us know her condition as soon as possible.''

The captain of the opposing team crossed the diamond to talk to Dick and it was decided between them to play out the remainder of the game.

It soon became apparent that without Logan the team was short one male player.

"Do you think your friend would mind filling in?'' Dick asked somewhat sheepishly, glancing at Tate.

"I can ask.''

"No problem,'' Tate said and smiled lazily as he picked up Logan's discarded mitt and ran onto the field.

Although they'd decided to finish the game, almost everyone was preoccupied with the accident. They ended up winning, thanks to Tate, but only by a slight margin.

The group as a whole proceeded to the pizza parlor to wait for word about Patty.

Tate sat across the long wooden table from Abby, chatting easily with her fellow teammates. Only a few slices of the two large pizzas had been eaten. Their conversation was a low hum as they recounted their versions of the accident and what could have been done to prevent it.

Mentally, Abby was grateful for Logan's clear thinking and quick actions. He wasn't the kind of skilled softball player that would stand out on a team; but he gave of himself in a way that was essential to every member of the team. Only a few days earlier she'd found Logan lacking. Compared to the muscular Tate, Logan had appeared a poor second. Now she noted that his strengths were inner ones. Again she was reminded that if given the chance, she would love this man for the rest of her life.

Abby didn't see Logan step inside the restaurant, but the immediate clamor caused her to turn her head around. She stood with the others.

"Patty's fine," he assured everyone. "Her arm's broken, but I don't think that's news to anyone."

"When will she be back?"

"We want to send flowers or something."

"When do you think she'll feel up to company?"

Everyone spoke at once. Calmly Logan answered each question and when he finished, the mood around the table was considerably lighter.

Someone stuck a quarter in the jukebox and the melodious sounds of a Western ballad filled the restaurant.

A tingling awareness across the nape of her neck told Abby that Logan was near. With a sweeping action he swung his foot over the long bench and joined Abby at the table.

His eyes focused on Tate, sitting across from Abby. "I wish I could say it's good to see you again," Logan said with stark unfriendliness.

"Logan," Abby hissed, "please don't."

The two men eyed each other like bears who had violated each other's territory. Tate had no romantic interest in her, Abby was convinced of that, but Logan was openly challenging him and Tate wouldn't walk away from such blatant provocation.

Unaware of the dangerous undercurrents swirling around the table, Dick Snyder sauntered over and slapped Logan across the shoulders.

"We owe a debt of thanks to Tate here," he informed Logan cheerfully. "He stepped in for you when you were gone. He batted in the winning run."

Logan and Tate didn't so much as blink. "Tate's been doing a lot of that for me lately, isn't that right, Abby?"

Wrenching her gaze from him, Abby stood and squared her shoulders. With as much dignity and pride as she could muster, she walked out of the restaurant and returned home alone.

The phone was ringing when she walked into the apartment. Abby let it ring. She didn't want to talk to anyone.

"Abby, would you take the French bread out of the oven?" her mother called from the patio.

"Okay." Abby turned off the broiler and pulled out the cookie sheet on which oblong slices of French bread oozed with melted butter and tiny pieces of garlic. Her enthusiasm for this birthday celebration was nil.

The doorbell caught her by surprise. "Are you expecting anyone?" she asked her mother, who had returned to the kitchen.

"Not that I know of. I'll get it."

Abby was placing the toasted bread slices in a warming basket when she heard her mother's surprised voice.

Turning, Abby's gaze clashed with Logan's.

Chapter Six

A shocked expression crossed Logan's sober face. "Abby." He took a step inside the room and paused.

"Hello, Logan." A tense silence ensued as Abby primly folded her hands.

"I'll check the chicken," Glenna Carpenter murmured discreetly as she scooted past them.

"What brings you to this neck of the woods?" Abby forced a lightness into her voice, which wobbled indecisively. Beyond the shocked surprise, his face displayed an underlying troubled look. Tiny lines fanned out from his eyes as if he hadn't been sleeping well. For that matter neither had Abby, but she doubted that either would admit as much.

Logan handed her a wrapped package. "I wanted your mother to give you this. But since you're here—happy birthday."

A small smile parted her trembling lips as Abby accepted the brightly wrapped gift. He had come to her parents' home to deliver this, but he hadn't expected her to be there.

"Thank you." She continued to hold it.

"I didn't expect to see you." He stated the obvious.

"Where else would I be on my birthday?"

Logan shrugged, standing stiff with obvious discomfort. "With Tate."

Abby released a breathless sigh of indignation. "I thought I'd explained that I'm not involved with Tate. We're friends, nothing more."

"Then why see him?" he demanded, his voice low and troubled.

Frustrated anew, Abby shook her head and dropped her gaze. They'd gone over this issue before. Another argument wouldn't help. It could only hurt, and Abby had endured enough emotional turmoil in the past few weeks to last years.

"Abby." Logan's voice was deadly quiet. "Don't you see what's happening? You may not think of Tate in a romantic light, but I saw the way he was looking at you in the pizza parlor."

"You openly challenged him." Abby threw out a few challenges of her own. "How did you expect him to react? You wouldn't have behaved any differently," she stated. "And if you've come," she added as she sucked in a quivering breath, "if you've come tonight to ruin my birthday...then you can just leave. I've had about all I can take from you, Logan Fletcher." She whirled around not wanting to face him.

"I didn't come for that." The defeat was back in his voice again.

The quiet in the room was deafening. Abby's pulse thundered through her ears as she waited for the sounds of him leaving, at the same time hoping that he wouldn't.

"Aren't you going to open your present?" he said at last.

Abby turned and wiped away a lone tear that had escaped from the corner of her eye. "I already know what it is," she said, glancing down at the package. "Honestly, Logan, you're so predictable."

"How could you possibly know?"

"Because you got me the same perfume last year for my birthday." Deftly she removed the wrapping paper and held up the small bottle of expensive French fragrance.

"I like the way it smells on you," Logan murmured, walking across the room. He lightly rested his hands on the rounded curve of her shoulders. "And if I'm so predictable, you'll also recall that there's a certain thank-you I expect."

Any resistance drained from her as Logan gently pulled her into his embrace. Tenderly he parted her lips and with a small, happy moan, Abby slid her arms around his neck and tasted the sweetness of his kiss. A wonderful languor stole through her limbs as his mouth brushed the sweeping curve of her lashes and burned a trail down her cheek to her ear.

"I love you, Logan," Abby whispered with all the intensity of her emotions.

Logan went utterly still. Gradually he raised his head so he could study her. Unflinching, Abby met his gaze determined that he see for himself what her eyes and heart were saying.

"If you love me, then you'll stop seeing Tate," he stated flatly.

"And if you love me, you'll trust me."

"Abby." Logan stroked his fingers through his hair, abruptly dropped his hands and stepped away. "I . . ."

"Oh, Logan." Glenna Carpenter moved out of the kitchen. "I'm glad to see you're still here. We insist you stay for dinner. Isn't that right, Abby?"

Logan held her gaze with mesmerizing simplicity.

"Of course we do. If you don't have another appointment," Abby stated meaningfully.

"You know I don't."

Abby knew nothing of the kind, but didn't want to argue. "Did you see the gift Logan brought me?" Abby asked her mother and held out the perfume.

"Logan is always so thoughtful."

"Yes, he is," Abby agreed and slipped an arm around his waist, enjoying the feel of him at her side. "Thoughtful, but not very original." Her eyes smiled into his, pleading with him that for tonight they could forget their differences.

Logan's arms slid just as easily around her. "But with that kind of thank-you, what incentives do I have for shopping around?"

Abby laughed and led the way to the back patio.

Frank Carpenter, Abby's gray-haired father, was busy standing in front of the barbecue, basting chicken.

"Logan," he exclaimed and held out a welcoming hand. "This is a pleasant surprise. It's good to see you."

Logan and her father had always gotten along and shared several common interests. For a time that had irked Abby. Defiantly she had wanted to make it clear that she wouldn't marry a man solely because her parents thought highly of him. Her childish attitude had altered dramatically these past weeks.

Abby's mother brought another place setting from the kitchen to add to the three already set at the picnic table. Abby made a couple more trips into the kitchen to carry out the salad, toasted bread and a tall glass of iced tea for Logan.

Absently, Logan accepted the frosty glass from her and smiled, already deep in conversation with her father. A happiness washed over Abby as she munched on a potato chip. Looking at the two of them now—Abby busy helping her mother and Logan chatting easily with her father—there was little to distinguish them as unmarried.

Dinner and the time that followed were cheerful. Frank suggested a game of cards while they ate birthday cake and ice cream. But Abby's mother immediately rejected the idea.

"I think Glenna's trying to tell me to keep my mouth shut because it's obvious you two want some time alone," Abby's father complained.

"I'm saying no such thing," Glenna denied instantly as an embarrassed flush brightened her cheeks. "We were young once, Frank."

"Once!" Frank scolded. "I don't know about you, woman, but I'm not exactly ready for the grave."

"We'll play cards another time," Logan promised, diverting a friendly argument between her parents.

"Double-deck pinochle," Frank prompted. "Best card game there is. Just ask the missus."

Glenna pretended to agree but dramatically rolled her eyes when Frank wasn't looking.

"Shall we?" Logan successfully contained a smile and held out his open palm to Abby. She placed her hand in his, more contented than she could ever remember being. After their farewells to her parents, Logan followed her back to her apartment, parking his car next to hers. He took a seat while Abby hurried into the next room.

"Give me a minute to freshen up," Abby called out as she ran a brush through her hair and studied her reflection in the bathroom mirror. She looked happy. The sparkle was back in her eyes.

On impulse she dabbed some of the perfume Logan had given her to the pulse points at the hollow of her throat and her wrists. Maybe this would bring out the animal in him. He wasn't one to display a lot of emotion, but he seemed to be coming along nicely in that area. His kisses had produced an overwhelming physical response in Abby, and she was aware that his feeling for her ran deep and strong. It had been only a matter of weeks ago that she'd wondered why he bothered to kiss her at all.

"I suppose you're going to suggest we drive to Des Moines and back," Logan teased when she joined him a few minutes later.

"Logan!" she cried, feigning excitement. "That's a wonderful idea."

He groaned and laid out the newspaper on the sofa. "How about a movie instead?"

Abby gave a fake groan. "So predictable."

"I've been wanting to see the latest Spielberg one."

"I've already been," Abby tossed back, not thinking. That was the movie she'd seen with Tate.

"When?"

Abby could feel the hostility exuding from Logan. He knew. Without a word he guessed that Abby had been to the movie with Tate.

"Not long ago." She tried desperately to put the evening back on an even keel. "But I'd see it again. The film's great."

The air between them became heavy and oppressive.

"Forget the movies," Logan said and neatly folded the paper. He straightened and stalked to the far side of the room. "In fact, why don't we forget everything."

Hands clenched angrily at her side, Abby squared her shoulders. "If you ruin my birthday, Logan Fletcher, I don't think I'll ever forgive you."

His expression was cold and unreadable. "Yes, but there's always Tate."

A hysterical sob rose in her throat, but Abby managed to choke it off. "I . . . I told you tonight that I loved you." Her voice wobbled treacherously as her eyes pleaded with his. "Doesn't that mean anything to you? Anything at all?"

Logan's gaze raked her from head to foot. "Only that you don't know the meaning of the word. I know you, Abby. You want both Tate and me. But you can't decide between us so you'd prefer to keep us both dangling until you make up your mind." His voice gained volume with each word. "But I won't play that game."

Abby breathed in sharply as a fiery anger burned in her cheeks. Once she would have ranted, cried and hurled her own accusations. Now she stood stunned and disbelieving. "If you honestly believe that, then there's nothing left to say." Her voice was unbelievably calm and more level than she dared hope. Life seemed filled with ironies all of a sudden. Outwardly she presented a clear-headed composure while on the inside she experienced a fiery pain. Perhaps for the first time in her life she was acting completely selflessly, and this was her reward—loosing Logan.

Without another word, Logan walked across the room and out the front door.

Abby watched him leave with a sense of unreality. This couldn't be happening to her. Not on her birthday. Last year Logan had taken her to dinner at L'Hôtel Sofitel and given her—what else—perfume. A hysterical bubble of laughter slipped from her. He was predictable, but so loving and caring. She remembered how they'd danced until midnight and taken a stroll in the moonlight. Only a year ago, Logan had made her birthday the most perfect day of her life. But this year he was ruining it.

Angry, hurt and agitated, Abby paced the living-room carpet until she thought she'd go mad. Usually when she was upset she'd ride her bike or do something physical. But bike riding at night could be dangerous, so she changed into old jeans and a faded sweatshirt that had a drawing of a Disneyland Cinderella's castle on the front. She had trouble locating her tennis shoe, then threw it aside disgustedly when the rainbow-colored lace snapped in two. There should be a law somewhere that said everything was supposed to be perfect on your birthday. No one should argue with the person they loved on their special day. It wasn't right!

But, then, nothing had gone right today. Tate had been disappointed that she wasn't going to be able to meet him. Because of his attitude, she'd gone to her parents' fighting off a case of guilt. Then Logan had shown up and everything had steadily and rapidly gone downhill.

Ripping a shoelace from one of her baseball shoes, Abby was forced to wrap the long strings around the sole of the shoe several times. On her way out the door, she paused and returned to the bathroom. If she was going to jog, then she'd go running smelling better than any other jogger in Minneapolis history. The perfume had been dabbed on every exposed part of her body when she stepped out the door.

A light drizzle had begun to fall. Terrific. A fitting tribute to a rotten day, Abby mused, disheartened all the more.

The first block was a killer. Heavens, she couldn't be that badly out of shape. She rode her bike a lot. And wasn't her running speed the best on the team? Maybe not; she couldn't remember.

The second block, Abby forced her mind off how out of breath she was becoming. Logan buying her perfume caused a chuckle to rise. "Predictable." "Reliable." "Intense." They were all words that adequately described Logan. But so were "unreasonable" and "stubborn", attributes she'd only seen recently.

The drizzle was quickly followed by a cloudburst and Abby's hair and clothes were plastered against her in the swirling wind and rain. She shouldn't be laughing. But she did anyway as she raced back to her apartment. It was either laugh or cry, and laughing seemed to come naturally. Laughing made her feel better than succumbing to tears. Laughing in the rain was far more difficult than venting her tears.

By the time Abby returned to her apartment, she was drenched and shivering. With her chin tucked in and her arms folded around her middle, she battled off the chill and hurried across the parking lot. Abby was almost at her door when she realized she didn't have the key. She'd locked herself out!

What more could go wrong? she demanded, slapping her hands defeatedly against her wet sides. Maybe the apartment manager was home. She stepped out in the rain to see if the lights were on in his apartment, which was situated above hers. Naturally his place was dark. Why not? That was the way everything else was going.

Cupping one hand over her mouth while the other held her stomach, Abby's laughter was mixed with sobs of anger and frustration.

"Abby?" Logan's urgent voice came from the street. Hurriedly he ran across the busy street, took one look at her and hauled her into his arms.

"Logan, I'll get you wet," she cried, trying to push herself free.

"What happened? Are you all right?"

"No. Yes. I don't know," she murmured and sniffled miserably. "What are you doing here?"

Logan brought her out of the rain and stood with his back blocking the wind, trying to protect her from the storm. "Let's get you inside and dry and I'll explain."

"Why?" she asked and wrung the water from the hem of her sleeve. "So you can hurl insults at me?"

"No," he denied vehemently. "I've been half-crazy wondering where you were."

"I'll just bet," Abby taunted unmercifully. "I'm surprised you didn't assume I was with Tate."

A grimace tightened his jaw, and Abby knew she had hit her mark. "Are you going to be difficult, or are we going inside and talk this out reasonably?"

"We can't go inside," she explained.

"Why not?" He was quickly losing his patience.

"Because I forgot my key."

"Oh, Abby," Logan groaned.

"And the manager's gone. Do you have any more bright ideas?"

"What about Dano?"

"Dano," Abby cried in disbelief. "At a time like this you're worried about my cat?"

"Did you leave the bedroom window open for him?" he asked with marked patience.

"Yes, but—" A glimmer of an idea sparked and she smiled boldly at Logan. "Follow me."

"Why do I have the feeling I'm not going to like this?" he asked under his breath as Abby pulled him by the hand around to the back of the building.

"Here," she instructed, bending her knee and lacing her fingers together to give him a boost upward to the half-open window.

"You don't expect to launch me through there, do you?" Logan glared at her, his eyes wide with shock. "I won't fit."

Rivulets of rain seeped down the back of Abby's neck. "Well, I can't. You know I'm afraid of heights."

"Abby, be reasonable. The window's hardly five feet off the ground."

"I'm standing here, drenched and miserable," she stormed, waving her hands wildly, slicing the night. "On my birthday, no less," she added sarcastically, "and you don't want to rescue me."

"I'm not in the hero business," Logan argued as he hunched his shoulders forward to ward off the rain. "Try Tate."

"Fine," she stormed, "I'll do that."

"Abby?" He sounded unsure as she dragged an aluminum garbage can to the side of the building.

"Get away!" she shouted. "I don't need you."

"What's the difference if you go through the window with a garbage can or have me lift you through?"

"Plenty." She wasn't sure what, but she didn't want to take the time to figure it out. All she wanted was a hot bath and ten gallons of hot chocolate.

"You're being totally irrational."

"I've always been irrational. It's never bothered you before." Her voice trembled as she balanced her weight on the lid of the garbage can. She reached the window and opened it enough to crawl through when she felt the garbage can lid give way. "Logan," she screamed, terror gripping her as she started to fall.

Instantly he was there. His steel arms gripped her waist as she tumbled off the aluminum container. Together they went crashing to the ground. Logan twisted so he received the brunt of the fall.

"Are you okay?" he asked frantically, straightening and brushing the hair from her face.

Abby was too stunned and breathless to speak, so she nodded.

"Now listen," he whispered angrily. "I'm going to lift you to the windowsill and that's final. Do you understand?"

Numbly she nodded.

"I've had enough of this arguing. I'm cold and wet and I want to get inside and talk some reason into you." He stood and wiped the mud from his hands against the side of his pants. "Come on." He gave her a hand and helped her up. Assuming the position she had taken earlier, he crouched and gave her his knee as a helping step as his laced fingers boosted her to the level of the window.

Abby fell inside the bedroom with a loud clunk, knocking the lamp off her nightstand.

"Are you okay?" Logan yelled from outside.

Abby stuck her head outside the window. "Fine. Come around to the front and I'll let you in."

"I'll meet you at the front door."

"Logan." She leaned forward and called, stopping him. She smiled at him provocatively. "You can be my hero any day of the week."

He didn't look convinced. "Sure. Whatever you say."

Abby had the front door unlocked and open by the time he came around the building. His wet hair was dripping water down his face, and his shirt was plastered to his chest, revealing a lean, muscular strength. He looked as drenched and miserable as she felt.

"You take a shower while I drive home and change out of these." He looked down ruefully over his mud-splattered beige pants and rain-soaked shirt.

Abby nodded in agreement. Logan had turned and was halfway out the door when Abby called him back. "Why are you here?" she questioned, wanting to delay his leaving.

He shrugged and gave her that warm, lazy smile she loved. "I don't know. I thought there might be another movie you wanted to see."

Abby laughed and blew him a kiss. "I'm sure there is."

Abby was humming a different kind of tune when Logan returned forty minutes later. Her hair was washed and blown-dry and hung in a long French braid down the middle of her back. She'd changed into a multicolored bulky sweater and purple cords.

Logan took one look at her and shook his head.

"Now what?"

"You clash. Not a single thing you have on matches."

"Well, for heaven's sake, I'd rather have my clothes clash than fight with you."

Logan cocked his head at an inquiring angle. "What's that got to do with anything?"

Abby smiled. "I don't know. It just sounded good. We're not going to fight, are we?"

"I certainly hope not!" he exclaimed forcefully. "I don't think I can take much more of this. When I left here the first time I was actually thinking..." He paused and scratched his head with one finger. "My mind was entertaining the thought of driving to Des Moines and back.''

"That's crazy." Abby tried unsuccessfully to hide her giggles.

"You're telling me?" He sat on the sofa and held out his arm to her, silently inviting her to join him.

Abby settled on the sofa, her head resting on his chest while his hand cupped her shoulder. His chin rested on the top of her head, his warm breath fanning her crown.

"Do you recall how uncomplicated our lives were just a few weeks ago?" Logan asked her softly.

"Dull. Ordinary, everyday people."

"What changed all that?"

Abby was hesitant to bring Tate's name into the conversation. "Life, I guess," she answered in general. "I know you may misunderstand this," she added in a husky murmur, "but I don't want to go back to the relationship we shared then." He hadn't told her he loved her and she hadn't realized the depth of her own feelings. More than that; she appreciated Logan as a valuable friend.

He remained still. "No, I don't suppose you would."

Abby repositioned her head and placed the palm of her hand on his jaw, turning his face so that she could study him. Their eyes met and his dark eyes watched her. The hard, uncompromising look disturbed her. Desperately she wanted to assure him of her love. But she'd realized after the first time that words were inadequate. She shifted and slid her hands over the hardness of his chest to pause at his shoulders.

The bold brilliance of his eyes searched her face. "Abby." He groaned her name as he fiercely claimed her lips. His hand found its way to the nape of her neck, his fingers gently pulling dark strands free from the braid so that he could twine the tresses through his fingers.

His breathing was deep and ragged when he buried his face in the gentle slope of her neck. "Just let me hold you for a while. Let's not talk."

She agreed and settled in the warm comfort of his embrace. The staccato beat of his heart gradually returned to a normal pace and Abby felt content and loved. The key to a peaceful relationship was to bask in the glow of their love for each other and not say a word. A smile dimpled her cheeks.

"What's so amusing?" Logan asked, his breath stirring the hair at the side of her face.

"How do you know I'm smiling?"

"I can feel it."

Abby tilted her head back so she could look into his eyes. "That's an interesting observation." How did one feel a smile? she wondered.

"Can I see you tomorrow?"

"If you weren't going to ask me, then I would have been forced to make some wild excuse to see you." Lovingly Abby continued to rub her hand along the side of his jaw, enjoying the slightly prickly feel of his beard against her skin.

"What would you like to do?"

"I don't care as long as I'm with you."

"My, my," he murmured and his hand took hers. Tenderly he kissed her palm. "You're much easier to please than I remember."

"You don't know the half of it," she teased provocatively.

Logan stiffened and sat upright. "What is tomorrow?"

"The tenth. Why?"

"I can't, Abby. I've got something scheduled."

A rush of disappointment caused her to raise her head. If she was frustrated, then so was Logan. "Don't worry, I'll survive," she assured him, then smiled lovingly. "At least I think I will."

"But don't plan anything for the day after tomorrow."

"Of course I'm planning something."

"Abby." He sounded tired and impatient.

"Well, I'm planning to spend the entire evening with you. I thought that was what you wanted."

"I do."

The grimness about his mouth relaxed.

It could have been her imagination, but almost immediately afterward, Logan appeared restless and uneasy. Later, as she dressed for bed, she was convinced it was her imagination.

The lesson with Tate the following afternoon went well, although Abby felt somewhat uneasy. She decided that what Logan didn't know wasn't going to hurt him. Tate's progress was remarkable as he advanced more quickly than any student she had ever tutored. From experience, she knew he was spending many hours each day studying, to be advancing at such a rapid rate.

On her way back to her apartment, Abby decided on the spur of the moment to stop off and see how Patty was recuperating. She'd mailed her a get-well card and had promised then to stop over some afternoon. Patty needed friends and Abby was feeling more than generous. Her topsy-turvy world had been righted and she felt wonderful.

Patty's married sister answered the doorbell.

"Hi, you must be from the office. Patty's gotten a lot of company. Everyone's been wonderful."

Abby wasn't surprised. Most everyone from the office complex where they both were employed was warm and friendly.

"This must be her day for company. Come on in. Logan's with her now."

Chapter Seven

Abby was dismayed as the sound of Patty's laughter drifted into the entryway, but she followed Patty's sister into the family recreation room.

Patty's broken arm was supported by a white linen sling and she sat opposite Logan on a long sofa. Her eyes were sparkling with undisguised happiness. Logan had his back to Abby, and it was all she could do not to turn around and leave. Instead she forced a bright smile onto her lips and made an entrance any Hollywood actress would envy. "Hello, everyone."

"Hi, Abby, what a pleasant surprise." Patty had never looked happier or, for that matter, prettier. Not only was her hair combed and styled, but she was wearing light makeup, which added color to her pale cheeks and accented her pretty brown eyes. Her dress and shoes were obviously new.

"How are you feeling?" Abby prayed the phoniness in her voice had gone undetected.

Logan stood up and came around the couch. His eyes didn't meet Abby's probing gaze.

"Hello, Logan, it's good to see you again."

"Hello, Abby."

"Sit down, please." Patty pointed to an empty chair with her good hand. "We've got a few minutes before dinner," Patty seemed oblivious to the finely strung tension between her guests.

"No thanks." Abby murmured and faked a smile. "I can only stay a minute. I just wanted to drop by and see how you were doing."

"Wonderful!" Patty exclaimed enthusiastically. "This is the first night I've been able to go out. Logan's taking me to dinner at l'Hôtel Sofitel."

Abby breathed in sharply and clenched her fist until her nails cut into her hand. Logan had taken her there only once, but Abby considered it their special restaurant. He could have taken Patty anyplace else in the world and not have it hurt as much as this one.

"Everyone's been wonderful," Patty continued. "Dick and his wife were over yesterday, and a few others from the team dropped by and brought me presents."

"We all feel terrible about the accident." Abby made her first honest statement of the visit.

"But it was my own fault." Patty chatted easily as Logan stood stiff and uneasy on the other side of the room.

Abby lowered her eyes, unable to meet the happy glow on Patty's. A crumpled piece of wrapping paper rested on the small table at Patty's side. It was the same paper Logan had used to wrap Abby's birthday gift the day before. He wouldn't have gotten Patty perfume. He wouldn't dare.

"You look so nice," Abby murmured. Her pulse quickened. What had Logan brought Patty? She had to know. "Is that a new scent of perfume you're wearing?"

"Yes, as a matter of fact Logan—"

"Hadn't we better be going?" Logan said as he made a show of glancing at his watch.

Patty looked slightly flustered. "Is it that time already?"

Following her cue, Abby glared at Logan and took a step in retreat. "I have to be going." A contrived smile curved her mouth upward. "Have a good time."

"I'll walk you to your car," Logan volunteered tightly.

Walking backward Abby made elaborate gestures with her hands, swinging them at her sides to give a carefree impression. "No, that isn't necessary. Really. I'm capable of finding my own way out. I was a Girl Scout, you know."

"Abby." Logan murmured under his breath.

"Have a wonderful time, you two," Abby continued, her voice only slightly high-pitched and strained. "I've only been to l'Hôtel Sofitel once. The food was great, but I can't say much for my date. But I no longer see the fellow. A real ordinary guy, if you know what I mean. And so predictable."

"I'll be right back." Logan directed his comment to Patty and gripped Abby by the elbow so hard that he half-lifted her off the carpet.

"Let me go," she seethed and tossed him a steaming glare.

Logan's grip relaxed once they were outside the house. "Would you let me explain?"

"Explain?" She threw the word in his face. "What could you possibly say? No." Wildly, she waved her hand in front of his chest. "Don't say a word. I don't want to hear anything you have to say. Do you understand? Not a word."

"You're being irrational again," Logan accused, apparently having difficulty keeping his rising temper in check.

"You're right," she agreed. "I've completely lost my sense of decency. Please forgive me for being so closed minded." Her voice was surprisingly even but it didn't disguise the hurt or the feeling of betrayal she was experiencing.

"Abby." Defeat caused his shoulders to hunch forward.

"Don't," she whispered achingly. "Not now. I can't talk now."

"I'll phone you later."

She consented with an abrupt nod, but at that point, Abby realized, she would have agreed to anything for the opportunity to escape.

Her hand was shaking so badly that she had trouble sliding the car key into the ignition. This was crazy. She felt secure in his love one night and betrayed the next.

Abby didn't drive to her apartment. The last thing she wanted to do was sit alone on a Saturday night. To kill time, she visited the Walker Art Center and did some shopping, buying herself a new outfit that she knew Logan would hate.

The night was dark and overcast as she let herself into the apartment. Hanging the jumpsuit with the paratrooper zipper bottoms, Abby recognized that spending this much money on one outfit was ridiculous. Her reasons were just as childish. But it didn't matter; she felt a hundred times better.

The phone rang the first time at ten. Abby ignored it. When it started ringing at ten-minute intervals, she simply unplugged it. There was nothing she had to say to Logan. When they spoke she wanted to feel composed. Tonight was too soon.

Calm now, she changed into her pajamas and sat on the sofa, brushing her long hair in smooth, even strokes. Reaction would probably set in tomorrow, but for now she was too angry to think.

When the doorbell chimed, Abby hesitated, then continued with her brushing and didn't miss a stroke.

"Come on, Abby, I know you're in there." Logan shouted from the other side of the door.

"Go away. I'm not dressed," she called out sweetly.

"Then get dressed."

"No," she yelled back.

Logan's laugh was breathless and bitter. "Either open up or I'll tear the stupid door off the hinges."

Just the way he said it convinced Abby this wasn't an idle threat. And to think only a few weeks ago she'd seen Logan as unemotional. Laying her brush aside, she walked to the door and unlatched the safety chain.

"What do you want? And for heaven's sake, keep the noise down; you're disturbing the neighbors." Abby was amazed she could sound so indifferent.

"If you don't let me in to talk to you, I'll do a lot more than wake the neighbors."

Abby couldn't remember a time she'd seen Logan display so much passion. Perhaps she should have been thrilled, but she wasn't.

"Did you and Patty have a good time?" she asked with heavy sarcasm.

Logan glanced briefly at his hands. "I had a reasonably nice time."

"I apologize if I put a damper on your evening in any way," she returned with smooth derision. "Believe me, had I known of your date, I would never have visited Patty at such an inopportune time. My timing couldn't have been better or worse, depending on how you look at it."

"Abby," he sighed heavily. "Let me in. Please."

"Not tonight, Logan." Her voice was barely above a whisper, but it was coated with steel. She had no intention of letting him into her apartment in her present state of mind.

Frustration furrowed his brow. "Tomorrow, then?"

"Tomorrow," she agreed and started to close the door. "Logan," she called and he immediately turned back. "Without meaning to sound like I care a whole lot, let me ask you something. Why did you give Patty the same perfume as me?" Some perverse part of herself had to know.

His look was filled with defeat. "It seemed the thing to do. I knew she'd enjoy it, and to be honest, I felt sorry for her. Patty needs someone."

Abby's chin quivered as the hurt coursed through her. Pride dictated that she maintain a level gaze. "Thank you for not lying," she said softly and closed the door.

Tate was waiting for her when Abby entered the park at eleven-thirty the next morning. Since she was no longer meeting Mai-Ling, Abby devoted time on the weekend to tutoring Tate.

"You look like you just stepped out of the dentist's chair," Tate declared, studying her closely. "What's the matter? Didn't you sleep well last night?"

She hadn't.

"Why didn't you let me take you to dinner the other night?" Tate chastised her gently. "You work too hard. You're always striving to help others."

Abby sat on the blanket Tate had spread out on the lush grass and lowered her gaze so that her hair fell forward in a lovely silken wreath. "I don't do nearly enough," she disagreed. "Tate," she said and raised her eyes expectantly to his. "I've never told anyone the reason we meet. Would you mind if I did? Just one person?"

Unable to sleep, Abby had tossed around the reasons Logan had asked Patty out for dinner. She was convinced he hadn't purposely meant to hurt her. The only logical explanation her mind accepted was the he wanted her to experience the same feelings he had, knowing she was continuing to see Tate. And yet he had gone to pains so that she wouldn't know about the dinner date. Nothing made sense anymore. But if she could tell Logan the reasons she was meeting Tate, things would be much easier for them both.

Tate rubbed a weary hand over his brow and eyes. "This is causing problems with you and—what's-his-name—isn't it?" He said it as if he couldn't bring himself to utter Logan's name. Until recently, the two held a grudging respect for each other. Now that, too, seemed to have changed.

Abby didn't want to put any unnecessary pressure on Tate so she shrugged her shoulders, hoping to give the impression of indifference. "It isn't bad. But I don't think he understands."

"Is it absolutely necessary that he know?"

"No, not really." Abby had known it would be extremely difficult for Tate to let anyone else in on his inability to read—especially Logan.

"Then would it be so selfish of me to ask that you don't say anything?" Tate questioned hesitantly. A look of pain flashed over his face, and Abby realized anew how hard it was for him to talk about his problem. "I suppose it's a matter of pride."

Abby's smile cracked her tense mouth. The relationship between the three of them was a mixed-up matter of pride—pride in a triangle.

"No, I don't mind," she replied, and opened her backpack to take out the latest series of books. "By the way, I want to give you this. She handed him three of her favorite Dick Francis books. "These may be a bit difficult for you in the beginning, but I think you'll enjoy them."

Tate turned the copy of *The Danger* over and read the back cover blurb. "His business is kidnapping?" He sounded unsure as he raised his eyes to hers.

"Trust me."

"I'll give it a try. But it looks a bit thick."

"Practice makes perfect."

Tate laughed in the low, lumbering, lazy manner she enjoyed so much. "I've never known anyone who has an automatic comeback the way you do." He took a cold can of soda and tossed it to her. "Let's drink to your wit."

"And have a celebration of words." She settled her back against the trunk of a massive elm and closed her eyes as Tate haltingly read the first lines of the pamphlet she'd given him. It seemed impossible that only a few weeks before he'd been unable to identify the letters of the alphabet. But his inability wasn't attributed to any learning disability, such as she had encountered in the past with others. She found that his capacity to sight-read was phenomenal. He was already at a junior level and advancing so quickly she had trouble keeping him in material. Unfortunately, his writing and spelling skills were advancing at a slower pace. Abby calculated that it wouldn't take more than a month or two before she could set him on his own with the promise to help when he needed any. Already he'd voiced his concerns about an application he would be filling out for the bank to obtain a business loan.

Abby hadn't been home fifteen minutes when Logan showed up, but for all the emotion he revealed, his face might as well have been carved in stone.

"Are you going to let me in today?" he asked, standing on the other side of her door.

"I suppose I'll have to."

"Not necessarily. You could make a fool of me the way you did last night."

"Me?" she gasped. "You don't need me to make you look like a fool. You do a bang-up job of it yourself."

His mouth tightened as he stepped into her apartment and folded his frame on the sofa.

Abby sat as far away from him as possible. "Well?" She was determined not to make this easy.

"Patty was in a lot of pain when I was driving her to the hospital the night of the accident," he began uneasily.

"I suppose a broken arm causes a fair amount of discomfort," she added sarcastically.

Logan's gravelly voice was cutting and indifferent. "I was talking to her fast and furious, trying to take her mind off how much she was hurting. Apparently, in all the garble I rashly mentioned I'd take her to dinner."

"I also suppose you also—rashly—suggested l'Hôtel Sofitel?" She felt chilled by his aloofness and she wasn't going to let him get off lightly.

An awkward silence followed. "I don't remember that part, but apparently I did."

"Apparently so," she returned with forced calm. "Maybe I could forget the dinner date, but not the perfume. Honestly, Logan, that was a rotten thing to do."

Hard impatience shadowed his tired features. "It's not like you're thinking. I got her cologne."

"For heaven's sake," she said exasperated. "Can't you be more original than that?"

"But it's the truth."

"I know that. But you can't go through life giving women perfume and cologne every time the occasion calls for a gift."

"All right, the next time I go buy a woman a gift, I'll take you along."

"The next time you buy a woman a gift," she interrupted with a stern, hard voice, "it had better darn well be me."

He ignored her statement. "Abby, how could you believe I care for Patty?"

She opened her mouth and closed it again. "Maybe I can believe that you really care for me. But I've seen the way Patty looks at you. It wouldn't take more than a word to have her fall in love with you. I don't want to see her hurt." Or any one of them for that matter, Abby mused. "It isn't like you to use Patty to make me jealous."

"I'm glad you realize that much." He breathed out his relief.

"But I recognize the looks she's giving you, Logan. She wants you."

"And Tate wants you!"

Abby's shoulders sagged in defeat. "Don't go bringing him into this discussion. It's not right. We were talking about you, not me."

"Why not? Isn't turnabout fair play?" The contempt in his expression made her want to cry.

"That's tiddlywinks, not love," she returned saucily.

"But if Patty looks at me with lovelorn eyes, then it can only mirror the way Tate sees you."

"Now you're being ridiculous." She shook her head in wonder at his irrational logic.

Slowly Logan rubbed his chin. "It has always amazed me that you can twist a conversation any way you want."

"That's not true," she denied, hating the way he was able to turn the situation around to suit himself.

"All right, let's put it this way: if you mention Patty, then I mention Tate. That sounds fair to me."

"Fine." She flipped a strand of hair over her shoulder. "I won't mention Patty again."

"Are you still seeing him?"

"Who?" Abby's eyes rounded innocently.

Logan's jaw tightened grimly. "I want you to promise me that you won't date Tate again."

Abby stared at him, dumbfounded.

"A simple yes or no. That's all I want."

The answer wasn't even difficult. She wasn't dating Tate now, but Logan didn't know that. "And what do I get in return?"

He bent his head to study his hands. "Something that has been yours for over a year. My heart."

At his words, all Abby's defensive anger melted. "Oh, Logan," she whispered, emotion bringing a misty happiness to her eyes.

"I've loved you so long, Abby, I can't bear to lose you." There could be no doubt of his words. Confirmation was boldly written in the shining light of his eyes.

"I love you, too." Her voice grew husky with the admission.

"Then why are you on the other side of the room when all I want to do is hold and kiss you?"

The deep well of tenderness inside her overflowed. She rose from the sitting position. "In the interests of fairness I think we should meet halfway. Agreed?"

He chuckled as he stood, coming to her, but his eyes revealed a longing that was deep and intense. A low groan rumbled from his throat as he swept her into his arms and held her as if he never wanted to let her go. He kissed her eyes, her cheeks, and nibbled at the corner of her mouth until she moaned and begged for more.

Abby's arms strained against him, wanting to be held closer and tighter, wanting to give more of herself as a natural outpouring to her love—a love so all-encompassing that it tore at her heart.

"Abby." His voice was muffled against her hair. "You're not going to sidestep my question?"

"What question?" She smiled against his throat as she gave him nibbling, biting kisses.

His hands gripped her shoulders as he pulled her slightly away from him so he could look down and study her face. "You won't be seeing Tate again?"

That wasn't what he asked, but she was afraid if she made an issue of his choice of words it would only cause further misunderstanding and a heated argument. "I promise never to date anyone else again. Does that satisfy you?"

He linked his hands at the small of her back and smiled deeply into her eyes. "I suppose it'll have to."

"Now it's your turn."

"What would you like?"

"First hold up your fingers. You were a Boy Scout, weren't you? I want Scout's honor here."

He did as she requested, his eyes sparkling with amusement.

"No more dating Patty."

"Agreed," he replied without hesitation.

"Inventive gift ideas."

He hesitated. "I'll try."

"You're going to have to do better than that."

"All right, all right, I agree."

"And—"

"There's more?" he interrupted in mocking impatience.

"And at some point in our lives I want to drive to Des Moines."

"Fine. Shall we kiss and seal this agreement?"

"I think it would only be proper," Abby commented eagerly as she slid her arms around his waist and fit her body to his.

His large hands framed her face, lifting her lips to meet his descending mouth. The kiss lacked the urgency of their first kiss, but was filled with a promise that was gentle and sweet. His breathing was ragged and deep when he released her, but Abby noted that her own wasn't any more even.

Not surprisingly, their truce held. Maybe it was because they both wanted it so badly. Sunday they met for breakfast which Abby cooked herself. Later, they drove over to Abby's parents' house and during the visit Frank Carpenter speculated that the two would be married by the end of the year. A few not-so-subtle questions about the "date" popped up here and there in the conversation. But neither of them seemed to mind. Logan was included in Abby's every thought. This was the way love was supposed to be, Abby mused as they returned to her apartment.

After changing clothes, they rode their bikes to the park and ate a picnic lunch. Later, with Logan's head resting in her lap, Abby leaned against the tree and closed her eyes. This was the same tree that had supported her back yesterday with Tate. A guilty sensation attacked the pit of her stomach, but she successfully fended it off.

"Did you hear that Dick Snyder was thinking of climbing Mount Rainier this summer?" Logan asked unexpectedly, his eyes closed as he chewed lazily on a long blade of grass.

In addition to softball, Dick's passion was mountains. She'd heard sketchy rumors of his latest venture, but hadn't been interested one way or another.

"I heard he was thinking about it," she replied lazily.

"What did you think?"

"What did I think about what?" Abby asked teasingly.

"They need an extra man. It sounded like the expedition would be cancelled otherwise." Logan was so serious. His brow was marred with a heavy frown as he looked up at her.

"Climbing the highest mountain in Washington State should be a thrill. They won't have trouble finding someone. Personally, I have trouble making it over speed bumps," she teased lovingly. Her hand brushed the hair from his forehead as she leaned forward to gently kiss his brow. "What's wrong?"

He smiled up at her and raised his hands to direct her mouth to his. "What could possibly be wrong?" he muttered thickly as he moved his mouth onto her lips for a kiss that left her breathless and reeling with the effect.

The next week was the happiest of Abby's life. Logan saw her daily. Monday they went to dinner at the same Mexican restaurant Tate had taken her to weeks before. The food was good, but Abby's appetite wasn't up to par. Again, Abby placed the twinge of guilt at the back of her mind. Tuesday he picked her up for class, but they decided to skip school. Instead they sat in the parking lot and talked until it was too late. From there they drove until they found a café where they could enjoy their soft drinks outside. The communication between them had never been stronger.

Tate phoned Abby at work the following Wednesday and asked her to meet him at the park after work. He wanted to be sure the application for the business loan had been filled out correctly. Uneasy about being seen in public with him for fear Logan would hear about it, Abby promised to stop off at his garage.

Later, when Logan picked her up for the softball game she was short-tempered and restless.

"What's the matter with you tonight?" he complained as they reached the park. "You're as jumpy as a bank robber."

"Me?" She feigned innocence. "Nervous about the game, I guess."

"You?" He looked at her with disbelief. "Miss Confidence? You better tell me what's really bothering you. Own up, kid."

Color blossomed in her pale cheeks. "Nothing's wrong."

"Abby, I thought we had come a long way recently. Won't you tell me what's bothering you?"

Logan was so sincere that Abby wanted to kick herself. "Nothing. Honest," she lied and swallowed at the expanding knot in her throat. She hated this deception, no matter how minor.

"Obviously you're not telling the truth," he insisted, and a telltale muscle twitched in his jaw.

"What makes you say that?" She gave him a look of pure innocence, amazed at what a good actress she was becoming.

"No gum. This is the first game I can recall that you haven't had a wad of bubble gum in your mouth."

"I forgot, that's all."

He released a low breath. "Okay, if that's the way you want it."

Patty was in the bleachers when they arrived, and waved eagerly when she saw Logan. Abby doubted that the girl noticed Abby was with him.

"Your girlfriend's here," Abby murmured sarcastically.

"My girlfriend is walking beside me," Logan muttered adamantly. "What's gotten into you lately?"

Abby released a jagged breath. "Don't tell me we're going to go over that again?" She didn't wait for him to answer. Instead she ran onto the field, shouting for Dick to pitch her the ball.

The game ran smoothly. Patty basked in the attention everyone was giving her and had the team sign her cast. Abby readily agreed to add her own comment, eager to see what Logan had written on the plaster cast. But she couldn't locate it without being obvious. Maybe he had done that on purpose. Maybe he'd written Patty a sweet message on the underside of her arm where no one else could read it. The thought was so ridiculous that Abby almost laughed out loud.

They lost the game by a slim margin, and Abby realized she hadn't been much help. During the get-together at the hamburger place afterward she sat and listened to the others joke and laugh. She wanted to join in the celebration, but deep inside she simply didn't feel like partying.

"Honey, are you feeling all right?" Logan sat beside her, holding her hand. He studied her with worried eyes.

"I'm fine," she answered and managed a halfhearted smile. "But I'm a little tired. Would you mind if we left?"

"Not at all."

They got up and, with Logan's hand at the small of her back, they made their excuses and left.

The silence in the car was deafening, but Abby did her best to ignore the gentle vibes Logan was sending her way. He didn't pry, but the questions hung in the air like pesky flies.

"How about if you let me cook your dinner tomorrow?" Abby volunteered brightly. "I've been terrible tonight and I want to make it up to you."

"If you're not feeling well maybe you should wait."

"I'm fine. Just don't expect anything more than hot dogs on a bun." She was only teasing and Logan knew it.

He parked outside her apartment and kissed her gently. Abby held on to him compulsively as if she couldn't bear to let him go. She felt caught in a game of cat and mouse between Tate and Logan—a game in which she was quickly becoming the loser.

The following evening, Abby was putting the finishing touches on a salad when Logan arrived.

"Surprise," he said as he held out a small bouquet of flowers to her. "Is this more original than perfume?" he asked with laughing eyes.

"Hardly." She gave him a soft brushing kiss across his freshly shaven cheek as she took the carnations from his hand. "Mmm, you smell good."

Logan picked a tomato slice out of the salad and popped it into his mouth. "So do you."

"Well, if you don't like the fragrance, you only have yourself to blame."

"Me? You smell like pork chops." He slipped his arms around her waist from behind and nuzzled her neck. "You know I could become accustomed to having you cook for me every night." The teasing quality left his eyes.

Abby dropped her gaze as her heart went skyrocketing into space. She knew what he was saying. The question had popped into her mind several times during the past few days. These feelings they were experiencing for each other were the kind to last a lifetime. Abby wanted to share Logan's life. The desire to wake up with him at her side every morning and cook their meals and give life to his children was stronger than any instinct. She loved this man and wanted always to be with him.

"I think I could become accustomed to being around," she admitted softly. "You do yard work, don't you?"

The doorbell chimed, breaking into their conversation. Impatiently Logan directed his gaze to the door. "Are you expecting anyone?"

"You," she teased. "Here, turn these. I'll see who it is and get rid of them." She handed him the spatula.

Abby's hand was shaking as she turned the knob, praying that it wouldn't be Tate. If she was lucky, she could ask him to leave before Logan knew what was happening.

Her worst fears were realized when she pulled open the door halfway.

"Hi."

"Hello, how are you?" she asked in a hushed whisper.

"I'm returning the books you lent me. I really enjoyed them." Tate gave her a funny look. "Is this a bad time, or something?"

"You might say that," she breathed. "Could you come back tomorrow?"

"Sure, no problem. Is it Logan?"

Abby nodded, and as she did so, the door was opened all the way.

"Hello, Tate," Logan greeted him stiffly. "I've been half-expecting you. Why don't you come inside where we can all visit?"

Chapter Eight

The two men regarded each other with open hostility.

Glancing from one to the other, Abby paused to swallow a lump of apprehension. Her worst fears had become reality. She wanted to blurt out the truth, explain to Logan exactly why she was seeing Tate. But one look at the two of them standing on either side of the door and Abby recognized the impossibility of making any kind of explanation. Like rival warlords, the two blatantly dared each other to make the first move.

Logan loomed at her side exuding bitterness, surprise, hurt and anger. He held himself still and rigid. Abby could feel the vibrations, as his body was close enough to touch.

"I'll see you tomorrow?" Tate spoke at last, making the statement a question. Ignoring Logan, Tate directed his gaze to Abby.

"Fine." Abby managed to find her voice, which was low and urgent. She wanted to scream at him to leave. If pride weren't dominating his actions, he would recognize what a horrible position he was placing her in. Apparently maintaining his pride was more important than the hurt he was causing her. Abby's eyes pleaded with Tate, but either he chose to ignore the silent entreaty or he didn't understand what her eyes were asking.

The enigmatic look in Tate's expression bounced off Logan and rested on Abby. "Will you be all right? Do you want me to stay?"

"Yes. No." She nearly shouted with frustration. He read the look in her eyes as a plea for help. This was crazy. This whole situation was unreal.

"Tomorrow, then," Tate said as he took a step in retreat.

"Tomorrow," Abby confirmed and gestured with her hand, begging him to leave.

Tate turned and stalked away.

Immobile, Abby stood where she was, waiting for Logan's backlash.

"How long have you been seeing each other?" he questioned with infuriating calm.

If he'd shouted and decried her actions, Abby would have felt better. But the composed manner with which he spoke relayed far more adequately the extent of his anger.

"How long, Abby?" he repeated.

Her chin trembled and she shrugged.

His short laugh was derisive. "Your answer says quite a bit."

"It's not what you think," she said hoarsely, desperately wanting to set everything straight.

His jaw tightened forbiddingly. "I suppose you're going to tell me that you and Tate are just good friends. If that's the case, then you can save your breath."

"Logan." Fighting back tears of frustration, Abby moved away from the door and turned to face him. "I'm asking you to trust me in this. Things are not always what they appear to be."

"Trust you!" His laugh was mocking. "I asked you to decide which one of us you wanted. You claimed you'd made your decision. You even went so far as to assure me you wouldn't be seeing Tate again." The intense anger darkened the shadows across his face, making the curve of his jaw abrupt and sharp.

"I said I wouldn't *date* him again," she corrected.

"Don't play word games with me," he threw back at her. "You knew what I meant."

Abjectly she agreed, with a feeble nod of her head.

"I suspected something yesterday at the game," Logan continued wryly. "That guilty look was in your eyes again. But I didn't want to believe what I was seeing. I refused to think about it."

Abby lowered her gaze at the onrush of pain. This deception hadn't been easy for her. But she was bound by her promise to Tate. She couldn't explain the circumstances of their meetings to Logan and salvage Tate's pride at the same time.

Logan's short laugh was bitter with irony. "Yet, when the doorbell rang I knew immediately it was Tate. To be honest, I was almost glad, because it clears away the doubts in my mind."

Determinedly he started for the door, but Abby's hand delayed him. "Don't go," she whispered. "Please." Her fingers tightened around his arm, wanting to bind him to her forever, starting with this moment. "I love you and . . . and if you love me, then you'll trust me."

"Love?" he repeated in a voice laced with contempt. "You don't know the meaning of the word."

Stunned, Abby dropped her hand and with a supreme effort met his gaze without emotion. "If that's what you think, maybe it would be better if you did leave."

Logan paused, his troubled expression revealing the inner storm raging within him.

"I may be wrong, but I was brought up to believe that love between two people constituted mutual trust," Abby added.

One corner of his mouth quirked upward. "And I assumed, erroneously it seems, that love constituted honesty."

"I . . . I bent the truth a little."

"Why?" he demanded. "No." He stopped her from explaining. "I don't want to know. Because it's over. I told you before that I wouldn't be kept dangling like a schoolboy while you made up your mind."

"But I can't explain now. I may never be able to tell you why."

"It doesn't matter, Abby, it's over," Logan stated starkly, his expression impassive.

Abby's stomach lurched with shock and disbelief. Logan didn't mean that. He wouldn't do that to them.

Without another word he walked from the room. The screen door slammed as he left the apartment. He didn't hesitate or look back.

Abby held out her hand in a weak gesture that pleaded with him to turn around and trust her. But he couldn't see her, and she doubted that it would have had any effect on him if he had. Unshed tears were dammed in her throat, but Abby held her head up in a defiant gesture of pride. The pretense was important for the moment, as she calmly moved into the kitchen and turned off the stove.

A mixed knot of laughter and tears caught in her throat. Only fifteen minutes before, she had lovingly stared into Logan's gaze, letting her eyes tell him how much she wanted to share his life. Now, swiftly and without apparent concern, Logan had severed her from his life as carelessly and thoughtlessly as he would an old pair of shoes. Yet Abby knew that wasn't true. He did love her. A thousand times she'd read it in his eyes. He couldn't hold her and kiss her the way he did without loving her. Abby knew him as well as he knew her. But then, Abby mused on a painful sigh, recently she doubted that Logan knew her at all.

Even worse was the fact that Abby recognized she was wrong. Logan deserved an explanation. But her hands were bound by her promise to Tate. And Tate had no idea what that pledge was doing to her and to her relationship with Logan. She couldn't believe that he would purposely do this, but Tate was caught up in his own trap. He viewed her as his friend and trusted teacher. He felt fiercely protective toward her, wanting in his own way to repay her for the second chance she was giving him by teaching him to read.

Logan and Tate had disliked each other on sight. The friction between them wasn't completely her fault, Abby realized. The ironic part was that for all their outward differences they were actually quite a bit alike.

When Abby had first met Tate that day in the park she'd found him compelling. She had been magnetically drawn to the same strength that unconsciously had bound her to Logan. Of course, these characteristics manifested themselves in different ways, but they were the same. This realization had taken Abby weeks to discover. And now, it seemed, the insight had come too late.

The weekend arrived in a foggy haze of emotional pain. Tate phoned Friday afternoon with the message that he wouldn't be able to meet with her because he was going to the bank to sign the final papers for his loan. He invited her out to dinner in celebration, but she readily declined. Not meeting him gave Abby a reprieve. She wasn't up to facing anyone at the moment. But each minute, each hour, the hurt grew less intense and life became more bearable. At least, that was what she tried to tell herself.

She didn't see Logan on Sunday, and forced herself not to search him out in the crowded park as she took a late-afternoon stroll. This was their day. Now it looked as if there wouldn't be any more lazy Sunday afternoons for them.

Involved in her melancholy thoughts, Abby realized that for the first time in recent history she'd come to Diamond Lake with only one purpose—exercise. She didn't want to see or talk to another soul. For someone who was usually so outspoken, Abby was quickly taking on the attributes of a loner.

Later that afternoon as the sun was lowering in a purple sky, Abby felt the gentle urge to sit on the damp earth and take in the beauty of the world around her. She needed the tranquility of the moment and the assurance that another day had come and passed and she had made it through the uncertainty, and was stronger for it. She'd never been weak, only headstrong and at times insensitive. But she was learning, and although the pain of that growth dominated her mind now, that too would fade. For several long moments Abby stared at the darkening sky and, for the first time in several long days, a peaceful assurance settled over her.

Sitting on the lush grass, her fingers splayed, enjoying the richness of the park grounds, Abby stared at the heavens. Those rare, peace-filled minutes soothed her soul and quieted her troubled heart. If she were never to see Logan again, she would always be glad for the good year they'd shared. In many ways Abby saw her own shortcomings. Too late, she had come to realize all that Logan meant to her and that she had carelessly tossed his love aside—with agonizing consequences.

The following afternoon Abby decided to contact Dick Snyder about Wednesday's softball game. Although she was dying for the sight of Logan, it would be an uncomfortable situation for them both.

"Dick, it's Abby," she spoke into the telephone receiver, suddenly feeling awkward and uneasy.

"Abby," Dick greeted her cheerfully. "It's good to hear from you. What's up?"

An involuntary smile touched the corners of her mouth. No-nonsense Dick. He climbed mountains, coached softball teams, ran a business with the effectiveness of a tycoon and thought of it all as a day's work for a day's pay. "Nothing much, but I wanted you to know I won't be able to make the game Wednesday."

"You too?"

"Pardon?" Abby didn't know what he meant.

"Logan phoned earlier and explained that he wouldn't be showing up for the game either. Are you two up to something we should know about?" he teased in an unaccountably playful mood. "Like running off and getting married?" he pried none too gently.

Abby felt the color flow out of her face. Her heart raced at double time. "No," she breathed, hardly able to find her voice. "That's not it at all."

Her hand was trembling when she replaced the receiver a couple of minutes later. So Logan had decided not to play Wednesday, either. If he'd decided against softball, she could assume he would also stop attending classes on Tuesday nights as well. The possibility of their running into each other at work was ever present. Their offices were only a half-block apart, but either he was going out of his way to avoid any possible meeting or he'd changed jobs as well.

Soon Abby's apartment became her prison. She did everything to take her mind off Logan, but as the days progressed, it became more and more difficult. As much as she didn't want to talk to anyone or make long explanations about Logan's absence, Abby couldn't tolerate another night alone. She had to get out.

Her intention had been to avoid her parents in an effort to elude their curiosity, but before she realized where she was headed, Abby pulled into their driveway.

"Hi, Mom," Abby said as she let herself in the front door.

Her father was reading the evening paper, and Abby paused at his side. She placed her hand on his shoulder and kissed him lightly on the forehead. "What's that for?" Frank Carpenter grumbled as his arm curved around her narrow waist and held her at his side. "Do you need another loan?"

"No money this time," Abby said with forced cheerfullness. "I was just thinking that I don't say I love you nearly enough." She glanced up at her mother. "I'm fortunate to have such good parents."

"How sweet," Glenna murmured softly, but her eyes were clouded with obvious worry. "Are you sure you're feeling all right? This isn't like you."

Abby successfully restrained the compulsion to cry out that nothing was right anymore. Not without Logan. She left almost as quickly as she came, making an excuse about the necessity of hurrying home to feed Dano. The weak explanation hadn't fooled her perceptive mother. Abby was grateful that Glenna didn't pry.

Another week passed and Abby didn't see Logan. Not that she expected she would. He was avoiding her as determinedly as she did him. Seeing him would only mean pain. She lost weight, and the dark circles under her eyes testified to her inability to sleep.

Sunday morning, Abby headed straight for the park, intent on finding Logan. Unconcerned at the emotional price, she was starving for him. Even a glimpse was sure to ease the pain she had suffered without him. She wondered if his face would reveal any of the same torment she had endured. Surely he regretted his lack of trust. He must miss her—perhaps even enough to set aside their differences and talk to her. And if he did, Abby knew she would readily respond. Abby's mind zoomed with skyrocketing speed as her thoughts played over the possible scenes. A thousand questions assaulted her, none of which seemed to have answers.

There had been a certain irony in her predicament. Tate had been exceptionally busy and she hadn't tutored him at all that week. He was doing so well now in his language-art skills that it wouldn't be more than a month before he would be reading and writing at an adult level. Once he'd completed the lessons, Abby doubted that she'd see him again. They had little in common and Tate had placed her on so high a pedestal that Abby doubted he'd ever see her as a woman. She was his goddess, and the position was an uncomfortable one. Abby only wanted to be herself and return to the carefree time when Logan was hers.

Abby sat toward the front entrance of the park so she wouldn't miss seeing Logan. She made the pretense of reading, but her eyes followed each person as they en-

tered the park. By noon, she'd been waiting three hours
and Logan had yet to arrive. Abby felt sick with disappointment. Logan came every Sunday morning to the
park. Certainly he wouldn't change that, too. And she
doubted that he would go so far to avoid seeing her. More
questions came to taunt her and still there were no answers.

Defeated, Abby closed her book and meandered down
the concrete pathway. She'd been sitting there since nine,
so she doubted that she'd missed him. As she strolled
through the park, Abby saw several people she knew and
paused to wave but walked on, not wanting to be drawn
into conversation.

Dick Snyder's wife was there with her two school-aged
children and called out Abby's name.

"Hi, come and join me. It'll be nice to have an adult
to talk to, for once." Betty Snyder chatted easily, patting
the seat of a empty chair. "I keep telling Dick that one of
these days I'm going mountain climbing and leave him
with the kids." Her smile was bright.

Abby sat on the bench beside Betty, deciding she could
do with a little conversation herself. "Is he at it again?"
she asked, already knowing the answer. Dick thrived on
challenge. Abby couldn't understand how anyone could
climb anything. Heights bothered her too much to consider anything as risky as scaling a mountain, or looking
out over a waterfall. She remembered once—

"Both Dick and Logan."

"Logan?" His name cut into her thoughts like a laser
gun and a tightness twisted her stomach. "He's not
climbing, is he?" The alarm in her voice rang out loud
and clear. Logan wasn't any mountaineer. Oh, he enjoyed a hike in the woods, but he'd never shown any interest in conquering anything higher than a sand dune.

Betty didn't bother to disguise her look of surprise. The coach's wife obviously assumed that Abby would know who Logan was with and what he was up to.

"Well, yes," Betty hedged. "I thought you knew."

"No." Abby swallowed tightly. "Logan hasn't said anything."

"He was probably waiting until he'd finished learning the basics from Dick."

"Probably," Abby replied weakly, her voice fading as alarm filled her. Pain and fear swelled in her breast. Logan climbing mountains? With a dignity she didn't know she possessed, Abby met Betty's gaze head on. It would sound ridiculous to tell Betty that this latest adventure had slipped Logan's mind. The fact was, Abby knew it hadn't. Briefly Abby recalled Logan telling her that Dick was looking for an extra man. But he hadn't said it as though he was considering doing it himself. The announcement had been casual, almost as if to ask her if she knew anyone who would be interested.

Betty continued, seeming to want to fill the stunned silence. "You don't need to worry. Dick's a good climber. I'd go crazy if he weren't. I have complete and utter confidence in him. You shouldn't worry about Logan. He and Dick have been spending a lot of time together preparing for this. Rainier is an excellent climb for a first ascent."

Abby heard nothing of Betty's pep talk and her heart sank. This had to be some cruel hoax. Logan was an accountant. He didn't possess the physical endurance needed to ascend fourteen thousand feet. He wasn't qualified to do any kind of climbing, let alone a whole mountain. Someone else should go. Not Logan.

Not the man she loved.

Her fingers were clenched so tightly that the blood supply to her fingers was severely hampered. This wasn't right! Oh, dear heavens, he was doing this for all the wrong reasons!

Betty's two rambunctious boys returned and closed around the two women, chatting excitedly about a squirrel they'd seen scoot up a tree. The minute it became possible, Abby slipped away from the family and hurried from the park. A heaviness weighted her chest. She had to get to Logan—talk some sense into him. The whole idea was ludicrous.

Abby returned to her apartment and climbed into her car. She drove around, seeking the nerve to confront Logan. He wouldn't be back until dark and possibly late. That didn't matter, she'd sit outside his apartment all night if she had to. Twice she drove to his place, but his parking space was empty.

After a frustrating hour in a shopping mall, Abby sat through a boring movie and immediately drove back to Logan's. For the third time she noted that he hadn't returned. She drove around again—for how long she was unsure. Time didn't matter. What did matter was Logan. Abby couldn't comprehend what had made him decide to do such a thing. A hasty decision wasn't like him. There was no deep-seated death wish in Logan. But if this crazy mountain-climbing expedition was his way of punishing her, he had succeeded beyond his expectation. The only thing left to do was to confront him.

Her decision made, Abby drove directly back to Logan's apartment. The sooner they got this settled the better. Relief washed over her at the familiar sight of his car.

His doorbell buzzed irritably. Abby could hear the nagging sound from the other side of the door. But Logan didn't respond. She pressed her finger against the bell so hard, the nail threatened to break. And still Logan didn't answer.

Abby decided she could sit this out if he could. Logan wasn't fooling her. He was there.

When the door was finally wrenched open, Abby lost her balance and stumbled ungracefully across the threshold. Regaining her balance, she turned and glared angrily at him.

"Abby." Logan removed the earphones from his head. "Have you been here long?" He moved aside and closed the door, placing the headset on top of the stereo. "I'm sorry I didn't hear you, but I was listening to a tape."

Regaining her composure, Abby straightened. "Now listen here, Logan Fletcher." She punctuated her speech with a finger pointed at him. With every word she spoke she pecked harder at his broad chest. "I know why you're doing this, and I won't let you."

"Abby, listen." He murmured her name in the soft way she loved.

"No," she cried unreasonable. "I won't listen."

He held her away from him, his hands cupping each shoulder. Abby didn't know if this was meant to comfort her or to keep her out of his arms. Desperately she wanted his arms, craved the comfort she knew was waiting for her there.

"You don't need to prove anything to me," she continued, her voice gaining volume and intensity. "I love you just the way you are. Logan, you're more hero than any man I know, and I can't—no," she corrected emotionally, "I *won't* let you do this."

"Do what?"

She looked at him in stunned disbelief. "Climb that stupid mountain."

"So you did hear. Damn. I was hoping none of this would get back to you."

"Logan," she gasped with hurt incredulity, "you weren't planning to let me know? You scheduled this entire escapade to prove some egotistical point to me and you weren't even going to let me know until it was too late? I can't believe that you'd do something like this. I simply can't believe it. You've always been so logical and all of a sudden you're falling off the deep end."

Now it was his turn to look flabbergasted. "Abby, sit down. You're becoming irrational."

"I am not," she denied hotly, but she did as he suggested. "Logan, please listen to me. You can't go traipsing off to Washington on this wild scheme. The whole idea is ludicrous. Crazy!"

He knelt beside her and she framed his face, her eyes pleading with his.

"Don't you understand," she reasoned. "You've never climbed before. You need experience, endurance and sheer nerve to take on a mountain. You don't need to prove anything to me. I love you just the way you are. Please don't do this."

"Abby." Logan said sternly and pulled her hand free, clenching her fingers to his chest. "This decision is mine. You have nothing to do with it. I'm sorry this upsets you, but I'm doing something I've been wanting to do for years."

"Haven't you listened to a word I've said?" She pulled her hands free and took in several deep, calming breaths. "You don't understand. You could be killed."

"You seem to be confusing the issues. My desire to make this climb with Dick and his friends has nothing to do with you and me."

"Nothing to do with you and me?" she repeated frantically. Had Logan gone mad? "If you think for one instant that I'm going to let you do this, then you don't know me, Logan Fletcher."

He stood up, and smoothed the side of his hair with one hand as he regarded her quizzically. "You seem to be under the mistaken impression I'm doing this to prove something to you."

"You may not have admitted it to yourself, but that's exactly the reason you are." The tremulous movement of her mouth scarcely resembled a smile. "You're climbing this crazy mountain because you want to impress me."

Logan's short laugh was filled with amusement. "I'm doing this, believe it or not, Abby, because I want to. My reasons are as simple as that. You're making it sound like I'm going before a firing squad. Dick is an experienced climber. Everyone has to start somewhere," he stated matter-of-factly.

"I don't believe you could be so naive," she stated flatly.

"Then that's your problem." His monotone took the sting from his announcement.

"But you could end up dead."

"I could walk across the street and be hit by a car tomorrow." Logan replied with infuriating calm.

Abby couldn't stand his quiet confidence another second. She leaped to her feet and stalked across the floor, gesturing wildly with her hands, unable to formulate her thoughts enough to reason with him. Pausing, she took several moments to compose herself. "If we discuss this in a rational manner you'll understand what I'm saying."

"Abby—"

"You're so caught up in the excitement of this adventure, you can't see it now," Abby interrupted, not wanting him to argue with her. He had to listen. He must.

Logan took her gently by the shoulders and turned her around. "I think you should realize that nothing you say is going to change my mind."

"I drove you to this—" her voice throbbed painfully.

"No," he cut in abruptly and brushed a hand across his face. "This is something I've always wanted to do. Abby, listen to me. You're making far more out of it than necessary."

Abby's head snapped up as a blazing blue fire in her eyes smoldered incredulously. "I don't believe that."

Logan breathed in harshly. "Unlike certain people I know, I don't bend the truth. It's true, Abby."

Abby's mouth twisted in a broken smile. "And you weren't even going to tell me."

His look was grudging. "From your reaction I think you can understand why."

Abby shut her eyes and groaned inwardly.

"Now if you'll excuse me, I really do need to study these tapes."

"I thought you were smarter than this. I've never heard of anything so stupid in my life," she stated waspishly. In her pain she was lashing out at him.

His smile was crooked and mirthless as if he'd expected that kind of statement from her.

"I'm sorry," she mumbled as she studied the scuffed-up toe of her shoe. The entire day had been crazy, she didn't know what she was thinking anymore. "I didn't mean that."

A finger under her chin lifted her gaze to his. "I know you didn't." For that instant all time came to a gentle halt. His eyes burned into hers with an intensity that stole her breath.

Of their own volition her hands slid over his muscular chest. She wound her arms around his neck and stood on the tips of her toes as she fitted her mouth over his. The slowburning fire of his kiss melted her heart. Every part of her seemed to be vibrantly alive. Her nerve endings tingled and flared to life.

Angrily Logan broke the kiss and pulled her arms free. "What's this?" he ground out harshly. "My last kiss before facing the firing squad?"

"Logan." She couldn't believe he'd torment her this way. "If you don't come back, I swear I'll never forgive you."

He rammed his hands into his pants pockets. Then, as if it was more than he could endure to look at her, he stalked to the other side of the room. "If I don't come back, it won't matter. We're not on speaking terms as it is."

From somewhere deep inside her, Abby found the strength to swallow her pride and smile. "That's something I'd like to change."

"No," he said without meeting her gaze.

"You're not leaving for two weeks. In that time you should be studying survival skills, not listening to tapes."

His low, harsh laugh sounded from across the room. "Perhaps."

"You won't be able to avoid seeing me," she ventured further. "I don't mind telling you that I plan to use every day of those weeks to change your mind."

"It won't work, Abby," he murmured confidently.

"But I can try, I—"

"I have two weeks before the climb, but we're flying in earlier to explore several mountains in the Cascade range."

"The Cascades?" Her voice throbbed with the shock of his statement. From school, Abby remembered that parts of the Cascade mountain range in Washington State had never been explored. He couldn't possibly be thinking of tackling some of those areas. Oh dear, this was even worse than she'd first suspected.

"My flight leaves tomorrow night."

"No," she mumbled miserably, the taste of defeat filling her senses.

"There's a whole troop who'll be seeing us off. If you're free you might want to come too."

Abby noted that he didn't ask that she come, but informed her of what was happening. Sadly she shook her head. "I don't think so, Logan. I refuse to be a part of any of it. Besides, I'm not much into tearful farewells and good wishes."

"I won't ask anything from you anymore, Abby."

"That's fine," she returned more flippantly than she intended. Involuntary tears glimmered on the fringes of her thick lashes. "But you'd better come back to me, Logan Fletcher. That's all I can say."

"I'll be back," he told her confidently.

Not until Abby was halfway home did she notice that Logan hadn't said he was coming back *to her*.

Later that night Abby lay in bed while a kaleidoscope of memories played through her mind. The most memorable scenes of her yearlong relationship with Logan flickered across the screen of her mind like mime characters. She had been so blind and so stupid not to have appreciated Logan. It had taken her almost a year to recognize how much she loved him.

Staring at the blank ceiling, a tear rolled from the corner of her eye and fell onto the pillow. Abby was intensely afraid for Logan.

The following afternoon, when Abby let herself into her apartment the telephone was ringing.

Abby's heart hammered in her throat as she lifted the receiver. Maybe Logan was calling to say goodbye. Maybe he'd changed his mind and would ask her to come to the airport after all.

"Hello?" She knew she sounded breathless, but it wasn't due to any physical exertion.

"Abby." Her mother's raised voice came over the line. "I just heard that Logan's joining Dick Snyder on his latest climb."

"Yes, mother," Abby confirmed in a shaky voice, wondering how her mother had found out about it. "His plane's leaving in—" She paused to check her wristwatch "—three hours, fifteen minutes, and twenty seconds. Not that I care."

"Oh, dear, I was afraid of that. You're taking this hard."

"Me? Why should I worry?" Abby attempted to sound as cool and confident as possible. She didn't want her mother to fret over her. But her voice cracked and she inhaled a quivering breath before she was able to continue. "He's in Dick's capable hands, Mother. All you or I or anyone can do is wait."

The hesitation was only slight. "Sometimes you amaze me, Ab."

"Is that good or bad?" Some of her sense of humor was returning.

"Good," her mother whispered. "It's very good."

The more Abby told herself she wouldn't break down and go to the airport, the more she realized there was nothing that could stop her.

A cold apprehension crept up her back and extended all the way to the tips of her fingers as Abby drove. Her hands felt clammy and cold, but her fingers were nothing compared to her stomach. The churning pain was almost more than she could endure. She hadn't been able to eat all day and was suffering the consequences. A tightness gripped the muscles of her throat, making speech almost impossible.

Abby arrived at the airport and the appropriate concourse in plenty of time to see the small crowd of well-wishers that surrounded Dick, Logan and company. Standing off to one side, Abby chose not to involve herself. She didn't want Logan to know she had come. Most everyone from the softball team was there, including Patty. The girl was more quiet and subdued than normal, Abby noted, and was undoubtedly just as worried about Logan's sudden penchant for danger as she herself was.

Once Abby thought Logan was looking into the crowd as if seeking someone. Desperately she wanted to run to him, hold him and kiss him before he boarded the aircraft. But she was afraid that she'd burst into tears and embarrass them both. Logan wouldn't want that. And her pride wouldn't allow her to show her feelings.

When it came time for Logan to board the airplane, there was a flurry of embraces, farewells and best wishes. Almost everyone departed as soon as the men were on the plane.

With her hands stuffed deep inside the pockets of the light jacket she wore, Abby watched at the window, hoping for the chance to see the plane airborne.

One by one the window seats filled up with passengers. Her heart was pounding so loud, it droned out the noise of the busy concourse.

When she thought she recognized Logan's boyishly-styled hair, her heart leaped to her throat. Raising her hand, she hoped the small action would catch his attention. The man she thought might be Logan turned and glanced back at the airport. But she had no way of knowing if it was him or whether he'd seen her or not.

Gently Abby touched her fingers to her lips and blew him a farewell kiss. She touched the window with her fingertips. Come back to me, she said with her eyes as the jetway was cleared and the plane started to roll away.

Chapter Nine

Abby rolled out of bed, stumbling into the kitchen and turned on the radio. The annual July heat wave was in full force and she was anxious to hear the weather report.

Cradling a cup of coffee in her hands, Abby eyed the calendar. In only a few days Logan would be home. Each miserable, apprehensive day brought him closer to her.

Betty Snyder continued to hear regularly from Dick about the group's progress as they trekked over some of the best and the worst of the Cascade mountains. Trying not to be obvious, Abby phoned Betty every other day or so, hoping to hear what information she could. Abby still didn't know the true reasons why Logan had joined this venture, but Abby believed they were all the wrong ones.

The first week after his departure, Abby received a postcard. She'd laughed and cried and hugged it to her breast as if it were an invaluable treasure map. Crazy, wonderful Logan. Anyone else would have sent her a scene of picturesque Seattle or at least the famous mountain he was about to climb. Not Logan. Instead he sent her a picture of a salmon.

His message had been impersonal:

How are you? Wish you were here. I saw you at the airport. Thank you for coming. See you soon.

Love, Logan

Abby treasured the card more than any bottle of expensive French perfume he had ever given her. Even when several others from the office shared similar messages, it didn't negate her pleasure. The postcard was tucked in her purse as a constant reminder of Logan. Not that Abby needed anything to jog her memory; Logan was continually in her thoughts. And although the message on the postcard was impersonal, Abby noted that he signed it with his love. It was a minor thing, but she held onto it with all her might. Logan did love her, and somehow, someway, they were going to overcome their differences because what they shared was too precious ever to relinquish.

"Disturbing news out of Washington State and climbers on Mount Rainier..." the radio announced.

Abby felt her knees go weak as she pulled out a kitchen chair and sat down. Immediately her hand fumbled with the knob as she turned up the volume.

"An avalanche of ice and snow has buried eleven climbers. The risk of another avalanche is hampering the chances of rescue. Six men from the Minneapolis area were making a southern ascent at the time of the avalanche. Details at the hour."

A slow, sinking sensation attacked Abby as she placed a trembling hand over her mouth.

At the top of the hour, the radio announcer continued to relate the sketchy details available about the avalanche and fatalities and concluded the report with the promise of an update later in the morning. Each word struck Abby like a body blow, robbing her lungs of vital oxygen. Pain constricted her chest. Fear, anger and a hundred emotions she couldn't identify were all swelling violently within her so that when the telephone rang, she nearly tumbled off the chair in her rush to answer it.

Please, oh, please don't let this be a call telling me Logan's dead, her mind screamed. *He promised he'd come back.*

"Abby, do you have your radio on?" Betty Snyder questioned urgently across the telephone line. Her usual calm manner had quickly evaporated with the disturbing report.

"Yes . . . I heard." Abby managed shakily. "Have you heard from Dick?"

"No," the soft voice trembled. "Abby, the team was making a southern ascent. If they managed to survive the avalanche, there's a possibility they'll be trapped on the mountain for days before a rescue team can reach them." Betty sounded as shocked and affected as Abby.

"We'll know soon if it's them."

"It's not them," Betty continued on a desperate note, striving for humor. "And if it isn't, I'll personally kill Dick for putting me through this. We should hear something soon."

"I certainly hope so."

"Abby," Betty asked with concern. "Are you going to be all right?"

"I'll be fine." But hearing the worry in her friend's voice did little to reassure her. "Do you want me to come over? I'll go crazy not knowing."

"Dick's mother is coming and she's a handful. You go on to the office and I'll call you as soon as there's any more news."

"Fine." Abby would have agreed to anything. Her friends in the office complex would need some reassurances themselves and Abby could relay quickly whatever messages came through.

"Everything's going to work out fine." Betty's tone was low and wavering and Abby realized her friend expected the worst.

The day had been a living nightmare when Abby thought about it later that afternoon. Every nerve was stretched taut and brittle. With every ring of the office phone her pulse thundered erratically before she could bring it under control and react normally.

Keeping busy was essential for her sanity those first few hours. But by a quarter to five she'd managed to settle her emotions. The worst that could have happened was that Logan was dead. The worst. And the radio had continued to report details that no one from the Minneapolis area was listed among those missing and presumed dead. But several climbing teams had yet to report. Abby decided there wasn't any need to face that possibility until necessary.

After work Abby drove directly to Betty's. The steps leading to the porch loomed before her like the mountain peaks Logan had climbed. Abby hadn't realized how emotionally and physically drained she was. But she forced herself to relax before entering her friend's home, more for Betty's sake than for her own.

"Have you heard anything?" she questioned calmly as Betty let her in the front door.

"Not a word." Betty's gaze studied Abby closely. "The worst part is not knowing."

Abby nodded and bit into her bottom lip. "And the waiting. I won't give up the belief that Logan is alive and well. He must be, because I'm breathing and living. If anything were to happen to Logan, a part of me would have died with him. My heart would know if he was dead." Abby recognized that her logic was refutable. Abby expected her friend to understand better than anyone else exactly what she was saying.

"I feel the same thing," Betty confirmed.

Abby stayed as long as she could before stopping off at her apartment to change clothes and watch the latest update on the evening news. The television reporter wasn't able to relate anything more than what had been available that morning.

Tate was waiting for her at the little Mexican restaurant where they met occasionally and raised his hand when she entered. Her relationship with Tate had changed in the past weeks. He had changed. Confident and secure now, he often came to her with minor problems. She was his friend as well as his teacher.

"I didn't know if you'd come or not," Tate said as he pulled out a chair for her. "I heard about the accident on Mount Rainier."

"To be honest, I wasn't sure I should come. But I would have gone crazy sitting at home brooding about it," Abby admitted.

"Any news about Logan?"

Abby released a slow, agonizing breath. "Nothing."

"He'll be fine," Tate said confidently. "He's quite a man. If anyone could take care of himself, I'd say it was Logan. He wouldn't have gone if he didn't know what to expect and couldn't protect himself."

Abby was surprised by Tate's insights. She would have thought, with the dark feelings between the two men, that Tate wouldn't be as generous in his comments.

"I thought you didn't like Logan," she broached the subject boldly. "It seemed that every time you two were around each other fireworks went off."

Tate lifted one shoulder with a dismissing shrug. "That was because I didn't like his attitude toward you."

"How's that?"

"You know. He acted like he owned you."

The problem was that Logan firmly held claim to her heart and it had taken Tate to show Abby how much she loved Logan. Her fingers circled the rim of the glass and she smiled into the ice water. "In a way he does," she whispered.

Tate picked up the menu and studied its contents. "I'm beginning to realize that. If there's anything I can do to patch things up between you two, you'll let me know, won't you?"

Abby reached across the table and squeezed his hand "Thanks, Tate."

The waitress approached their table. "Are you ready to order?"

Abby glanced at the menu and nodded. "I'll have the cheese enchiladas."

"Make that two," Tate instructed absently. "No." He paused. "I've changed my mind. I'll have the pork bur-rito."

Abby tried unsuccessfully to disguise her amusement.

"What's so funny?" Tate wanted to know.

"You. Do you remember the first few times we went out to eat? You always ordered the same thing I did. I'm pleased to see you're not still doing it."

"It was from force of habit. I owe you a great deal, Abby; more than I'll ever be able to repay."

"Nonsense." His gratitude sometimes made her uncomfortable. They were friends, and the basis of that friendship wasn't something they needed to discuss.

"Maybe this will help show a little of my appreciation." Tate pulled a small package from inside his pocket and handed it to her.

Abby was stunned, her fingers numb as she accepted the beautifully wrapped box. Her brow was creased in heavy lines as she raised her eyes to his. "Tate, please. This isn't necessary."

"Hush up and open your gift," he instructed, obviously enjoying her surprise.

When she pulled the paper away, Abby was even more amazed to note the name of a well-known and expensive jeweler embossed across the top of the case. Her heart was in her throat as she shook her head disbelievingly. "Tate," she began hesitatingly.

"Open it." An impish light glinted in his eyes.

Slowly she raised the lid to discover a lovely intricately woven gold chain that lay upon a bed of blue velvet. Even Abby's untrained eye recognized that the chain was expensive and of the highest quality. A small cry of undisguised pleasure escaped before she could hold back her amazement.

"Tate!" She could hardly take in the beauty of something so simple yet so elegant. For the first time in months she found herself utterly speechless.

"Cat got your tongue?" Tate teased.

"I can't believe it. It's beautiful."

"I knew you'd like it."

"Like it! Why, it's the most beautiful necklace I've ever seen. Thank you." Appreciation brightened her face as Abby raised her eyes to his. "But you shouldn't have, you know that, don't you?"

"If you say so."

"Now he's agreeable." Abby smiled as she spoke to the empty chair beside her. "Here, help me put it on."

Tate stood and came around to her side of the table. Gently he lifted the chain from its plush bed and laid it against the hollow of her throat. Abby dipped her head and lifted the wall of hair from the back of her neck to make it easier for Tate to hook the necklace.

When he returned to his chair, Abby felt a warm glow encompass her. "I still think you shouldn't have done this, but to be honest, I'm pleased you did. Nothing could be more perfect."

"I knew the minute I saw it in the jeweler's window that it was exactly what I was looking for. If you want the truth, I'd been searching for weeks for something special to give you. I want to thank you for everything you've done for me."

Abby didn't think Tate realized what a small part she had played in his tutoring. He had done all the real work himself. He was the one who spent hours learning to read and write. Gradually she had watched his progression from simple stories to a mature-adult reading level. He was the one who'd sought her out with a need and admitted his shortcoming—something he'd never been able to do before, always having hidden his inability. Abby doubted if Tate recognized how far he'd come from the day he'd followed her home from the park.

Later, when Abby undressed for bed, her hands fingered the simple chain, remembering Tate's promise. Maybe now he'd be willing to explain to Logan why Abby had met with him. The chain was her promise to patch things with Logan. In doing so, Tate would never realize how much this one gift meant to her.

Before leaving for work early the next morning, Abby phoned Betty in case there had been any news during the night. There hadn't been and discouragement sounded in Betty's voice as she promised to phone Abby's office if she heard any news regarding the men.

At about ten that morning, Abby had just finished updating the chart on a young teen who'd just visited the doctor, when she glanced up and saw Betty in the doorway that led from the reception area.

Abby straightened and stood immobile, her heart pumping at a furious rate. Suddenly, she went cold with fear. She couldn't move, or think. Even breathing became impossible. Logically, Betty would come to the office for only one reason. Logan was dead.

"Betty," she pleaded in a tortured whisper, "tell me. What is it?"

"He's fine...everyone is. They were stuck on the slopes an extra night, but made it safely to camp early this morning."

Abby closed her eyes and exhaled an anguished breath of pure release. Her heart skipped a beat as she moved across the room. The two women hugged each other fiercely as tears of happiness streaked their faces.

"They're on their way home. The flight will land sometime tomorrow evening. Everyone's planning to meet them at the airport. You'll come, won't you?"

In her anger and pain Abby had refused to see him off with the others...until the last minute. She wouldn't be so stubborn about welcoming him home. Abby doubted if she'd be able to resist hurling herself into his arms the instant he stepped off the plane. The mental image produced a lazy, contented smile. And once she was in his arms, Abby defied anyone to replace her.

"Abby? You'll come, won't you?" Betty's soft voice broke into her musings.

"I'll be there," Abby replied, as the mental image of their reunion played in her mind.

"I thought you'd want to be." Her friend gave her a knowing look.

Logan was safe and coming home. Abby's heart gave a sudden leap of excitement and she waited until it resumed its normal pace before returning to her desk.

"Tonight," Abby explained to Tate at lunch on Thursday. She swallowed a bite of the thick pastrami sandwich. "Word came yesterday that their flight will be arriving around nine-thirty. The office complex is planning a get-together with him and Dick on Friday night. You're invited to attend if you'd like."

"I just might come."

Tate surprised her with his easy acceptance. Abby had issued the invitation thoughtlessly, not expecting Tate to take her up on the offer. For that matter, it may even have been the wrong thing to do, since Logan was sure to be offended.

"I was beginning to wonder if you were ever going to invite me to any of those social functions your office group is always having."

"Tate." Abby glanced up, surprise written in the delicate features of her oval face. "I had no idea you wanted to come. Good grief, I'd be happy to include you. I wish you'd said something earlier. We're always looking for another single." Now she felt guilty for having excluded him in the past.

"Sure," Tate chimed defensively. "Those good people would take one look at a mechanic and decide they had something better to do."

"Tate, that's simply not true." And it wasn't. He would be accepted as would most anyone who wished to join them.

"It might cause a few heads to turn," Tate expelled his breath as if he found the thought amusing.

"Oh, hardly."

"You don't think so?"

Tate's lack of self-confidence was a by-product of his inability to read. Now that reading was no longer a problem, he would gain that maturity. Already she was seeing it evolve in him.

Moonlight flooded the ground. The evening was glorious. Not a cloud could be seen in the crystal-blue sky as it darkened into night. Slowly, Abby released a long, drawn-out sigh. Logan would land in a couple of hours and the world had never been more beautiful. She paused to hum a love ballad playing on the radio, thrilled at the romantic words.

In a matter of hours, Abby hoped she would be singing her own kind of love song—one composed especially for Logan.

She must have changed her clothes three different times, but everything had to be perfect. When Logan stepped off the plane and saw her, she wanted to look as close to an angel as anything he would find this side of heaven.

She spent an hour on her hair and makeup. Nothing satisfied her. Tight-lipped, Abby realized she couldn't make herself into an extraordinarily beautiful woman with what she had to work with. Sad but true. She could only be herself. She dressed in a soft, plum-colored linen suit and a pink silk blouse, with a rose pin, the same color as the outfit, placed at the top button. Dissatisfied with her hair, Abby pulled it free of the confining pins and brushed it until it shimmered and fell in deep natural waves that flowed down the middle of her back. Logan had always loved her hair worn loose, and would spend hours running his fingers through its glorious length.

A quick glance at her watch revealed that she was ten minutes behind schedule. Grabbing her purse, Abby was out the front door. Biting into the corner of her bottom lip she noticed that her car was running on "empty." Everything seemed to go wrong when she was late, especially when she was trying to be on time.

Abby pulled into a service station, splurging on the full service for once instead of pumping her own. *Hurry*, her mind screamed as the teenaged youth took his sweet time pumping the gasoline.

"Do you want me to check your oil, lady?"

"No," Abby snapped, handing him the correct change. "And don't wash the window. I haven't got time."

Inhaling deep breaths helped to take the edge off her impatience as Abby merged onto the freeway. A mile later an accident caused a minor slowdown.

By the time she arrived at the airport, her heart was racing at double time. A check at the airline counter revealed that Logan's flight was on schedule.

Abby's heels made clicking sounds against the polished floor as she half ran down the concourse. Within minutes the group from the office came into sight. She couldn't see Logan's plane land since she was so late.

An all-encompassing warmth stole over Abby as Logan came into view. His face was badly sunburned, the skin around his eyes white from his protective eye gear. He looked tanned and more muscular than she could remember. His eyes searched the crowd and paused on her, his look thoughtful and intense.

Abby beamed, wearing her brightest smile. He was so close. Close enough to reach out across the short distance and touch if it weren't for the people crowding around. Abby's heart swelled with the depth of her love. His own eyes mirrored the longing she was sure hers revealed. Those days apart were all either of them would need to recognize that they should never separate again.

Abby followed his progress in the line, edging her way toward him and Dick. The others who had come to greet Logan were chatting excitedly, but Abby heard none of their conversation. Logan was back. Here. Now. And she loved him. After today he would never doubt the strength of her feelings again.

In her desire to hurry and get to Logan, Abby nearly stumbled over an elderly gentleman. She stopped and apologized profusely, making sure the white-haired gentleman wasn't hurt. As she straightened, she heard someone call out Logan's name.

In shocked disbelief, Abby watched as Patty Martin flew across the room and dramatically threw herself into Logan's arms. Sobbing, she clung to him as if he'd returned from the dead. Soon the others gathered around and Dick and Logan were completely blocked from Abby's view.

The bitter taste of disappointment filled her mouth. Logan should have pushed the others aside and come to her. *Her* arms should be the ones around him. *Her* lips should be the ones kissing him. But all that had been denied her, and Logan didn't seem to care.

Proudly Abby decided that she wouldn't fight her way through the throng of well-wishers. If Logan wanted her, then she was here. And he knew it.

But apparently he didn't. Five minutes later the small party moved out of the airport receiving area and progressed in the direction of the parking lot. As far as Abby could tell, Logan hadn't so much as looked around to see where she was. Her disappointment at not being the first to greet him was far more palatable than his apparent indifference to her company.

After all the lonely days of waiting for Logan, Abby had a difficult time deciding if she should attend the small party to be held in the local smorgasbord place in his and Dick's honor the following evening. If he hadn't come to her at the airport, then what guarantee did she have that he wouldn't shun her a second time? The pain lingered from his first rejection. Abby didn't know if she could bear another.

To protect her ego on Friday night Abby dressed casually in jeans and a cotton top. She timed her arrival so that she wouldn't cause a stir when she entered the restaurant. As she'd expected, and as was fitting, Logan and Dick were the focus of attention while they relived their tales of danger on the high slopes.

Abby filled her plate and took a seat where she could see Logan plainly. She sincerely doubted that she could force down any dinner.

Sitting as she was in a convenient corner, Abby was able to observe Logan covertly. Every once in a while he would glance up and search the room. He seemed to be waiting for someone. Abby would have liked to believe he was looking for her, but she could only speculate. The tension flowed out of her as she witnessed again the strength and vitality that exuded from him. That experience on the mountain had changed Logan, just as it had changed her.

Unable to endure being separated a moment longer, Abby pushed her plate aside and crossed the room to his table. Logan's gaze locked with hers as she approached. Someone was speaking to him, but Abby doubted that Logan heard a word of what was being said.

"Hello, Logan," she said softly. Her hands hung nervously at her sides. "Welcome home."

"It's good to see you, Abby." His gaze lovingly roamed her face. He didn't need to pull her into his arms for Abby to know what he was feeling. It was all there for her to read. Her doubts, confusion and anxiety were all wiped out in one lingering moment.

"I'm sorry about what happened at the airport." His hand gripped hers. "There wasn't anything I could do."

Still their eyes held as she studied his face. Every line, every groove, was so lovingly familiar. "Don't apologize. I understand." Who would have believed a simple touch of someone's hand could cause such a wild array of sensations? Abby felt shaky and weak just being this close to him. An encompassing, tingling warmth ran up the length of her arm as he gently enclosed her in his embrace.

"Can I see you later?"

"You must be exhausted." She wanted desperately to be with him, but she could wait another day. After all these days, a few more hours wouldn't matter.

"Seeing you again is all the rest I need."

"I'll wait for you," she promised.

Dick Snyder tapped Logan on the shoulder and led him to the front row of tables. After a few words from Dick that highlighted part of their adventure, Logan stood and thanked everyone for their support. He relayed part of what he'd seen and the group's close brush with death.

The tables of friends and relatives listened enthralled as Logan and Dick spoke. Just hearing him casually tell of the adventure was enough to make Abby's blood run cold. She had come so close to losing him.

Abby stood apart from Dick and Logan while they shook everyone's hand as they filed out the door and thanked them for coming. When the restaurant began to empty Logan crossed the room and brought Abby to his side. Abby was grateful that Tate had phoned to explain he couldn't come. In an effort to assure him he'd be welcome another time, Abby invited him to the office picnic scheduled that weekend in Diamond Lake Park. Tate promised to make that if possible.

Logan led her into the semidarkened parking lot and turned Abby into his arms. A tormented look was in his eyes as he gazed down upon her upturned face.

"As crazy as it sounds, the whole time we were trapped on that mountain, I was thinking that if I didn't come back alive you'd never forgive me." With an infinite tenderness he brushed the hair from her face. He kissed her with a slow languor, as if he were dying for the taste of her, yet cautious not to take too much at once.

"I wouldn't have forgiven you," she murmured and smiled up at him in the dim light.

"Abby, I love you," he said with a wealth of emotion as he crushed her against his chest. "It took a brush with death to prove how much I wanted to come home to you."

His mouth sought hers and with a joyful cry, Abby wrapped her arms around him and clung. Tears of happiness clouded her eyes as Logan weaved his hands in the silken length of her hair. He couldn't seem to take enough or give enough as he kissed her again and again, rubbing his lips over and over her tender mouth. Finally he buried his face in the gentle slope of her neck.

His hands framed her face as he inhaled a steadying breath. "When I saw you standing across the hall tonight it was all I could do to be polite and stay with the others."

Abby lowered her gaze. "I wasn't sure you wanted to see me."

"You weren't sure?" Logan said disbelievingly. He slid his hands down to rest on the curve of her shoulders. His finger caught on the delicate gold chain and he pulled it up from beneath her blouse.

Abby caught her breath and went completely still. Logan seemed to sense that something wasn't right as his eyes searched hers.

"What's wrong?"

"Nothing. What could possibly be wrong?"

His eyes fell on the chain. "It's lovely and something far more expensive than you could afford. Who gave it to you, Abby? Tate?"

Chapter Ten

Abby pressed her lips so tightly together that her teeth hurt. "Yes, Tate gave me the necklace."

"You're still seeing him, aren't you?" Logan dropped his hands to his sides and didn't wait for her to respond. "After everything I've said and done, you still haven't been able to break off this relationship with Tate, have you?" The steely hardness in his voice seemed to reach out and slap her.

"Tate has nothing to do with you and me," she insisted and inhaled a sharp breath to hide the abject frustration. After the long, trying days of separation they couldn't argue! Abby wanted to cry out that she loved him and nothing else should matter. She should be able to be friends with a hundred men if she loved only him. Urgently Abby attempted to salvage their reunion. "I realize this is difficult for you to understand. To be honest, I don't know how I'd feel if you were to continue seeing Patty Martin."

The line of his mouth hardened with impatience. "Then maybe I should."

Abby realized Logan was tired and impatient, but an angry retort sprang readily to her lips. "You certainly seem to have a lot in common with Patty—far more than you do with me."

"The last thing I want to do is argue." The control Logan had on his anger sounded as fragile as Abby's.

"No, I agree, my intention in coming tonight wasn't to defend my actions while you were away. And yes," she paused to compose herself, knowing her face was flushed and her body was shaking, "I saw Tate."

The area became charged with an electric silence that seemed to spark and crackle. The air was heavy and still, pressing down on her like the stagnant air before a thunderstorm.

"I think that says everything I need to know," he said with quiet harshness.

Abby nodded sharply, forcing herself to meet his piercing gaze. "Yes, I suppose it does." She took a step backward.

"It was kind of you to come and welcome me back this evening." A muscle twitched in his jaw. "But as you can imagine, the trip was exhausting. I'd like to go home and sleep for a week."

"I can imagine." Her low voice was shaky. "Perhaps we can discuss things later."

Logan's face was hard, harder than she thought possible. "There won't be another time, Abby."

"That decision is yours," she returned calmly, although her voice trembled with reaction. "Good night, Logan."

"Goodbye, Abby."

Goodbye! Her mind shouted back. She knew what he was saying as plainly as if he'd screamed it at her. Whatever had been between them was completely over.

"I expect you'll be seeing a lot more of Logan now that he's back," Tate commented from her living room the following afternoon.

Abby brought out a sandwich from the kitchen and handed it to him before taking a seat. "We've decided to let things cool between us," she replied with as much aplomb as she could manage. "Cool" was an inadequate word. Their relationship was in Antarctica. They'd accidentally run into each other that morning while Abby was doing some grocery shopping and had exchanged a few polite, stilted sentences. After a minute Abby could think of nothing more to say.

"You know what I've decided?" Abby paid an inordinate amount of attention to the makings of her sandwich. "I've come to the belief that love is a highly overrated emotion."

"How's that?"

Abby didn't need to glance up to see the amusement in Tate's face. She shrugged and took the first bite of her lunch. How could she explain that from the moment she realized how much she loved Logan, all she'd endured was a deep and intense emotional pain. "I don't know," she said at last, regretting having brought up the subject.

"Abby?" Tate's look was thoughtful.

She leaped to her feet. "I forgot the iced tea." She hurried into the kitchen, hoping Tate would let the subject drop.

"Did I tell you the bank approved my loan?"

Abby's head perked up. "That's great."

"They phoned yesterday afternoon. Bressler's pleased, but not half as much as I am. I have a lot to thank you for, Abby."

"I'm really pleased for you," Abby said with a quick nod. "You've worked hard and deserve this." Abby knew how relieved Tate was that the loan had gone through. He'd called Abby twice from pure nerves just to have someone to talk through his doubts. Abby had a few of her own and listening to Tate helped. Tomorrow afternoon they were going to attend the picnic together and although Abby was grateful for Tate's friendship, she didn't want to give the wrong impression to her friends. Logan had already jumped to conclusions. There was nothing to say the others wouldn't just as easily. Tate was a friend—a special friend—but their relationship didn't go beyond that. It couldn't, not when she was in love with Logan.

Sunday afternoon Abby's thoughts were preoccupied when she dressed in shorts for the annual picnic. She was glad Tate was going with her, but she hoped Logan didn't do or say anything that would make them uncomfortable.

Logan. She paused as the unhappiness weighed upon her heart. Her thoughts were filled with him every waking minute. Even her dreams involved him. This misunderstanding, this lack of trust had gone on long enough. From the moment Logan had stepped off the plane, Abby had longed for Tate to explain the situation and heal her relationship with Logan. Abby had assumed that as time progressed they would naturally get back together. Now, just the opposite was proving true. With every passing hour, Logan was drifting further and further out of her life. Yet her love was just as strong. Perhaps even stronger.

Since Tate was meeting her at the park, Abby arrived early and found a picnic table for them. When Logan came, he claimed the table directly across from hers and Abby felt the first bit of encouragement since they last spoke. As quickly as the feeling came, it vanished. Logan worked, setting out the tablecloth and arranging the cooler on the table seat without so much as a glance her way. As he finished, a heaviness stole through her. Only a few feet separated her from Logan, but in some ways no distance had ever been greater. He gave no indication that he had seen her. Even her weak smile had gone unacknowledged.

Soon they were joined by the others, chatting and laughing. A few men played horseshoes while the women sat and visited. The day was glorious, birds trilled their songs from the tree branches and soft music played from a cassette tape. Busy putting the finishing touches on a salad, Abby's sweet voice blended with the music. The last thing in the world she felt like doing was singing, but if she didn't do something soon, she'd start crying.

Tate arrived and Abby could see by the way he walked and other telltale mannerisms that he was nervous. Some of the people he knew from the softball game. He looked surprised when one of the guys called out a greeting. The two men talked for a minute and Tate joined her soon afterward.

"Hi."

"There's no need to be nervous," she said, as a means of greeting.

"What? Me nervous?" he joked. "They're good people, aren't they?"

"The best."

"Even Logan?"

"Especially Logan."

Tate was silent for a moment. "I'll see what I can do to patch things up between you two."

Unhurriedly, she raised her gaze to his. "I'd appreciate that."

His returning smile of reassurance told her how difficult revealing his past would be. Abby hated to ask him to do it, but there didn't seem to be any other way.

Abby's heart was racing and she tightly laced her fingers and sat searching out Logan. He wasn't playing horseshoes or checkers with the older pair of gentlemen, but standing alone with his back to her, staring out over the still, quiet lake. Every part of her wanted to join him, but she knew that if she did go and stand by his side, he'd simply walk away.

Defeated, Abby spread out a blanket and stretched out on it, pretending to sunbathe. She must have drifted into a light sleep, because the low-pitched voices of Tate and Logan were what stirred her.

"Seems to me you've got the wrong table," Logan was saying. "Your girlfriend's over there."

"I was hoping we could talk."

"I can't see that there's much to talk about. Abby's made her decision."

The noise that followed sounded as though Logan was emptying his cooler onto the table and ignoring Tate as much as possible. Abby resisted the urge to roll over and see exactly what was happening.

"Abby's nothing more than a friend," Tate said next.

"You two keep claiming as much." Logan sounded bored and slightly impatient.

"It's the truth."

"Sure," Logan answered with a snicker.

A rustling sound followed and faintly Abby could hear Tate stumbling over the awkward words that listed the ingredients on the side of a soda can.

"What are you doing?" Logan asked with a heavy note of irritation.

"Reading," Tate explained. "And for me that's some kind of miracle. You see, until I met Abby here in the park helping Mai-Ling, I couldn't read."

A shocked silence followed his announcement.

"For a lot of unimportant reasons, I never properly learned," Tate continued. "Then I found Abby. Until I met her, I didn't know that there were good people like her who would be willing to teach me."

"Abby taught you to read?" Logan was stunned.

"I asked her not to tell anyone. I suppose that was selfish of me in light of what's happened between you two. I don't have any excuse except pride."

Someone called Logan's name and the conversation was abruptly cut off. Minutes later the announcement was made that it was time to eat. Abby joined the others, helping where she could. She and Tate were sitting with Dick and Betty when she felt Logan's eyes resting on her. The conversation going on around her faded away as Abby felt Logan's sharp gaze studying her. The space between them evaporated as she turned and boldly met his look. In his eyes she read anger, regret and a great deal of inner pain.

When it came time to pack up her things and head home, Abby found Tate surrounded by a group of singles on the lawn. He glanced up and caught Abby's eyes and waved. "I'll phone you later," he told her cheerfully, apparently surprised at the amount of attention he generated from the women.

"Fine," she assured him. She hadn't gotten as far as the parking lot when Logan caught up with her.

His hand cut into her shoulder as he turned her around. The anger she'd thought had been directed inward was now focused directly on her.

"Why didn't you tell me?" he demanded sharply.

"I couldn't. Tate asked me not to."

"That's no excuse," he shouted, then paused to inhale a shuddering breath and start again with controlled patience. "All the times I questioned you about meeting Tate, you were tutoring him. The least you could have done was tell me."

"I already told you that Tate was uncomfortable with that. Even now, I don't think you appreciate what it took for him to admit it to you," she explained slowly, enunciating each word so that there would be no misunderstanding. "I was the first person he'd ever told that he had a problem. Such a confession was a traumatic thing for him. I couldn't go around telling others. Surely even you can understand that."

"Traumatic for him! What about me? What about us?"

"My hands were tied. I asked you to trust me. A hundred times I pleaded with you to look beyond the obvious."

Logan closed his eyes and emitted a low groan. "How could I have been so stupid?"

"We've both been stupid and we've both learned valuable lessons. Isn't it time to put all that behind us?" She wanted to tell him again how much she loved him, but something stopped her.

Hands buried deep in his pockets, Logan turned away from her, but not before Abby saw that his eyes were narrowed in a deep frown. A proud mask stole over his expression, blocking her out.

Abby watched in disbelief. The way he was behaving, one would think she had been the unreasonable, untrusting one. The more Abby thought about their short conversation as she drove home, the angrier she got.

Pacing the carpet of her living room, she folded her arms around her waist to ward off a sudden chill. "Of all the nerve," she snapped at Dano who paraded in front of her. The cat shot across the room and out his escape route through her bedroom window—he was smart enough to know when to avoid his mistress.

Snapping her car keys out of her purse, Abby hurried outside. She'd be darned if she'd let Logan end things like this.

His car was outside his apartment. In her anger, her shoes made hard, clicking noises as she marched to his door and leaned heavily on the buzzer.

Logan swung the door open impatiently. "What's going on?"

She pointed her index finger at his stomach until he backed out of the doorway.

"Now listen here, Logan Fletcher. I've had about all I can take from you." Every word was punctuated with a jab of her finger against his chest. Logan stumbled backward.

"Abby? What's the problem?"

"You and that stubborn pride of yours."

"Me?" he shouted in return.

"When we're married, you can bet I won't put up with this kind of behavior."

"Married?" he repeated incredulously. "Who said anything about marriage?"

"I did." Her hand sliced the air.

"Doesn't the man usually do the asking?" he asked sarcastically.

"In this case I could see trouble ahead." Some of her anger was dissipating and she began to realize what a fool she was making of herself. "And . . . and while we're on the subject, you owe me an apology."

"You weren't entirely innocent in any of this," he barked.

"All right. I apologize. Does that make it easier on your fragile ego?"

"I also prefer to make my own marriage proposals."

Abby paled and crossed her arms. She wouldn't back down now. "Fine. I'm waiting."

Logan squared his shoulders and cleared his throat. "Abby Carpenter," his voice softened measurably, "I want to express my sincere apology for my behavior these past weeks."

"It's been over a month," she inserted with a low breath.

"All right, a month," Logan amended with obvious displeasure. "Although you seem to be rushing the moment, I don't suppose it would do any harm to give you this." He pulled a diamond ring from his pocket.

Abby nearly fell through the floor. Her mouth dropped and she was speechless as he lifted her hand and slipped the solitaire diamond on her ring finger. "I was on my way to your place," he explained as he pulled her into his embrace. His hands locked at the base of her spine as his gaze roamed lovingly over her shocked face. "I've loved you for a long time. I hadn't worked out a plan yet on how to steal your heart away from Tate. But you can be assured I wasn't going to let you go without a struggle."

"But my heart—"

His lips blocked out any explanation regarding the ownership of her heart. Abby released a small cry of wonder and wound her arms around his neck and gave herself to the kiss as his mouth closed over hers. Nothing had ever been so beautifully sweet as Logan's kiss. His mouth sought the corner of her eye, her nose, her ear, as if he couldn't get enough of her.

Gradually he raised his head, and his eyes were filled with the same magnificent wonder she was experiencing. "I talked to Tate again after you left the park," Logan said in a husky murmur. "I was a complete fool."

"No more than usual." Her small laugh was breathless.

"It'll take me at least thirty years to make it up to you."

"Make it forty and you've got yourself a deal."

His eyes smiled deeply into hers. "Where would you like to honeymoon?"

Abby's eyes sparkled with silent laughter. "Des Moines—where else?"

Silhouette Romance

COMING NEXT MONTH

UNHEAVENLY ANGEL—Annette Broadrick
With their inheritance at stake, Angel and Blake could either get married and produce an heir, or lose millions! Could an earthly union turn into a blessing in disguise?

MAGIC CITY—Lynnette Morland
Charlotte came to Miami for a vacation. But sun and relaxation seemed less appealing after she'd met Tony Devlin, producer of a popular TV show. Charlotte was ready to take action . . . with Tony.

AN IRRITATING MAN—Lass Small
When John returned to Indiana as a successful writer, he set his sights on Talullah Metcalf. But John had always driven her crazy. He was almost as irritating . . . as he was irresistible.

MIRAGE—Mary O'Caragh
Claire couldn't figure out what photographer Raleigh Durban was doing in Death Valley. But when he took an interest in her geological survey, she knew geology would never be the same.

THE RIGHT MOVES—Arlene James
To cowboy Rafferty Sharpstone, a rodeo was no place for a woman or for love. Angie didn't agree and was about to show him that he was wrong—on both counts.

AMENDED DREAMS—Glenda Sands
Born a farm girl, Rebecca always dreamed of the excitement of a bustling city. But then she met Dr. Lawrence Roth, a country veterinarian. Would she change her plans for the good doctor's love?

AVAILABLE NOW:

CHAMPAGNE GIRL
Diana Palmer

HERO IN BLUE
Terri McGraw

LAUGHTER IN THE RAIN
Debbie Macomber

GETTING PHYSICAL
Marie Nicole

THE PAINTED VEIL
Elizabeth Hunter

SWEET MOCKINGBIRD'S CALL
Emilie Richards

Silhouette Special Edition

AMERICAN TRIBUTE

AMERICAN TRIBUTE

Where a man's dreams count
for more than his parentage...

*Look for these upcoming titles
under the Special Edition
American Tribute banner.*

CHEROKEE FIRE
Gena Dalton #307—May 1986
It was Sabrina Dante's silver spoon that
Cherokee cowboy Jarod Redfeather couldn't
trust. The two lovers came from opposite
worlds, but Jarod's Indian heritage taught
them to overcome their differences.

NOBODY'S FOOL
Renee Roszel #313—June 1986
Everyone bet that Martin Dante and Cara
Torrence would get together. But Martin
wasn't putting any money down, and Cara
was out to prove that she was nobody's fool.

MISTY MORNINGS, MAGIC NIGHTS
Ada Steward #319—July 1986
The last thing Carole Stockton wanted was to
fall in love with another politician, especially
Donnelly Wakefield. But under a blanket of
secrecy, far from the campaign spotlights,
their love became a powerful force.

AM-TRIB-1R

Silhouette Special Edition

AMERICAN ✦ TRIBUTE

AMERICAN TRIBUTE

American Tribute titles now available:

RIGHT BEHIND THE RAIN
Elaine Camp #301–April 1986
The difficulty of coping with her brother's
death brought reporter Raleigh Torrence
to the office of Evan Younger, a police
psychologist. He helped her to deal with
her feelings and emotions, including love.

THIS LONG WINTER PAST
Jeanne Stephens #295–March 1986
Detective Cody Wakefield checked out
Assistant District Attorney Liann McDowell,
but only in his leisure time. For it was the
danger of Cody's job that caused Liann to
shy away.

LOVE'S HAUNTING REFRAIN
Ada Steward #289–February 1986
For thirty years a deep dark secret kept them
apart—King Stockton made his millions while
his wife, Amelia, held everything together.
Now could they tell their secret, could they
admit their love?